# A Plane and Simple Connection

# A Plane and Simple Connection

## ESKAY KABBA

4 Horsemen
Publications, Inc.

4 Horsemen Publications, Inc.
1497 Main St. Suite 169
Dunedin, FL 34698
4horsemenpublications.com
info@4horsemenpublications.com

Cover by J. Kotick
Typesetting by Autumn Skye
Edited by Kris Cotter

*Library of Congress Control Number: 2023931137*

*Paperback ISBN-13: 978-1-64450-836-7*
*Hardcover ISBN-13: 978-1-64450-842-8*
*Audiobook ISBN-13: 978-1-64450-840-4*
*Ebook ISBN-13: 978-1-64450-839-8*

# Table of Contents

Chapter 1 . . . . . . . . . . . . . . . . . . . . . . . . . . . . . . . . . 1

Chapter 2 . . . . . . . . . . . . . . . . . . . . . . . . . . . . . . . .18

Chapter 3 . . . . . . . . . . . . . . . . . . . . . . . . . . . . . . . .29

Chapter 4 . . . . . . . . . . . . . . . . . . . . . . . . . . . . . . . .47

Chapter 5 . . . . . . . . . . . . . . . . . . . . . . . . . . . . . . . . 68

Chapter 6 . . . . . . . . . . . . . . . . . . . . . . . . . . . . . . . 82

Chapter 7 . . . . . . . . . . . . . . . . . . . . . . . . . . . . . . . .97

Chapter 8 . . . . . . . . . . . . . . . . . . . . . . . . . . . . . . . 117

Chapter 9 . . . . . . . . . . . . . . . . . . . . . . . . . . . . . . .138

Chapter 10 . . . . . . . . . . . . . . . . . . . . . . . . . . . . . . .158

Chapter 11 . . . . . . . . . . . . . . . . . . . . . . . . . . . . . . .178

Chapter 12 . . . . . . . . . . . . . . . . . . . . . . . . . . . . . . .193

Chapter 13 . . . . . . . . . . . . . . . . . . . . . . . . . . . . . . .212

Chapter 14 . . . . . . . . . . . . . . . . . . . . . . . . . . . . . . .231

Book Club Questions . . . . . . . . . . . . . . . . . . . . . . . 245

Author Bio . . . . . . . . . . . . . . . . . . . . . . . . . . . . . .247

Content warning: Explicit Langauge,
Explicit Sexual Situations, and Drug Use.

*R*ion started counting down the last thirty minutes. He pulled his sweatshirt hoodie up close to his face and leaned farther into the small window. The guy next to him smelled like old eggs in cheap cologne. His tree trunk thighs were pressed against Rion's smaller ones, which he found amazing and frustrating, given the armrest between them. Three hours in the air with someone who made him physically and mentally recoil—the guy just wouldn't stop talking—was more than enough. The man was getting off in New York, and the plane was staying to refuel, and then new passengers would be boarding. Hopefully, his new seatmate would be someone who didn't spend the whole time talking about his ex-wife, who had left him because she felt like she outgrew him and he had stayed the same lazy, unambitious man he'd always been. By the end of his trip, Rion could honestly see why she had left him.

"...but when her mother gets in her ear, that's what happens. And her father never liked me, anyway. He always thought I was a meathead jock. But football was my life, and when I tore my ACL, what did they expect me to do? It's not like she supported me anyway," the man droned on.

It didn't matter that Rion had his headphones in and had long since turned away from him. Trevor, as he learned the man's name was before the plane took off, seemed like he just needed to let off some steam and hear himself talk. It was Rion's fault. He was a people person and liked starting conversations with interesting people. Most of the time, it was fine; even the most annoying people had interesting stories. But Trevor was not interesting. He was someone who expected things to just fall into his lap, and when they didn't, he took no accountability. Rion had no patience for people who didn't own their circumstances, good or bad.

"Ladies and gentlemen, please turn up your trays, adjust your seats to the upright position, and fasten your seatbelts," the flight attendant announced. "We will be landing in approximately twenty minutes."

*God, yes*, Rion thought. He quickly did as he was told while Trevor continued to talk about starting over and moving in with his cousin in Brooklyn, who owned an auto body shop and could use the help. How he had lived in San Francisco his whole life but was ready for a change, to get as far away from his lost love as possible. How he couldn't wait for the first snowfall and fighting with New Yorkers, who all sounded like Robert DeNiro to him.

"Sounds like it's going to be a good move for you," Rion answered happily, excited for Trevor to finally leave the plane.

Rion held onto the armrests tightly; already hating the landing more than the rising of the plane. As the aircraft descended, he closed his eyes, chewed his gum, and counted backward from fifty in his head until he felt the wheels bump against the tarmac. Only then did he open his eyes.

He looked at the bright lights from the airport. Rion had actually never been to New York. One day he'll write a story set there and be forced to roam the city that never sleeps, but it had never been a must-do on his list. Neither was London, for that matter, but between falling asleep during a Harry Potter marathon and waking up to a raging boner that had him looking up porn, a story formed in his head. He had spent the last week writing the outline and then knew he had to go. In order for the story to be successful, Rion had to understand the culture and see it for himself. So no, New York was not his destination today, London was. South London, Brixton, to be exact. He would start there.

"Thanks for listening, Ryan. Have fun on your trip," Trevor said as he pulled his bag down and followed others out of the aisle. Rion waved goodbye and didn't even bother correcting the pronunciation of his name.

When there were just a few stragglers like himself left on the plane, he stood up and stretched. He looked at his phone for the time: 11:37 p.m. The plan was to leave at 12:50 a.m., just enough time to refuel and get the red-eye passengers on. He was hoping a plane leaving in the middle of the night in the middle of the week would be empty, so he would be able to stretch out on the seat next to him for the next seven hours.

He sent his sister and best friend, Gabby, a text, letting her know that he was okay and would call when he got to London. After a few stretches and checking his Facebook and Instagram accounts, he started walking the length of the plane. His seat, 19A, was halfway toward the back of the plane and it was relatively empty, which was nice. He smiled at a young, Southeast Asian–looking woman who had a little girl sleeping on her lap. She had beautiful brown skin, black hair shaped in a bob, full, dark pink lips, and small, dark brown eyes. Her daughter looked just like her, down to the same haircut. He wanted to take out his camera and snap a picture, but he knew that would be rude. He walked down to the front, crossed the walkway, and walked up the other side of the plane. He smiled at other people and walked back to his seat. By the time he got there, new passengers were starting to board.

*And here we go*, Rion thought. He promised himself that whoever sat down, he would not start up a conversation. He wanted to write notes for his new writing project and sleep a little if he could. Rion continued standing and glancing down the aisle to see who would be sitting next to him, hoping no one would be. He happily watched people one by one find seats in front of him and behind him. Because he was watching so intently, he saw the man in the red shirt walk down the aisle first, looking down at his ticket and looking up at the numbers along the way.

As he got closer and closer, Rion couldn't help but stare at the very attractive man with a fair complexion and dirty blond hair that was shaved along the sides, full and long in the middle. He had blue eyes, a thin upper lip, and a full pink bottom lip. He kept biting his bottom lip as he looked around and finally his eyes caught Rion's. Rion wanted to stop staring, but now he couldn't. And neither could Red Shirt Guy. He came closer and stopped right in front of Rion, then looked around at the numbers. Red Shirt was taller than Rion, who was a good 6'1". He was so close Rion could smell his aftershave.

"I'm right here," he said softly, his voice a perfect tenor on the lower end.

Rion gave him a small smile and moved over to his seat by the window. But then the man looked up again and said, "Oh, sorry, I'm here. 19C, not 19B." He turned around and put his bag in the compartment across the aisle from him, then plopped down in his seat.

Rion realized he was still standing and staring. He slowly sat down in his seat and stared ahead at the back of the seat in front of him. Red Shirt did not look back at him. Instead, he pulled out his phone and started scrolling around. Rion laughed a little to himself. He clicked his seatbelt on, pulled out his notebook, and started jotting down ideas about his characters, namely changing the hair color of William to dirty blond instead of dark brown and having his heart-shaped lips become fuller on the bottom than on the top.

"Ladies and gentlemen, welcome to British Airways flight 636, non-stop to Heathrow Airport in London," the flight attendant began.

Rion looked around and saw that no one was sitting next to him, which made him gleeful. It was pretty empty where Red Shirt was, too. He turned back to his notebook and continued to write his description of William. Once the safety video went off, it was silent as everyone got ready for takeoff.

"I hope you know what you're doing," that deep voice he had heard ten minutes ago spoke again.

Rion looked up at him. "Excuse me?"

"You weren't paying attention. So if the flight goes down, I hope you know where all the exits are and how to find your mask."

Rion chuckled. "I've been on the same plane since San Francisco. I watched it once already. I think I'll be okay."

Red shirt shrugged. "Suit yourself. But when turbulence starts, don't look to me to save your ass."

Rion laughed out loud. "Wow, you're the opposite of a good Samaritan. I'll make sure to find my own way."

The man laughed, too. "I'm Nicholas. Nick." He held his hand out.

"Rion." Rion grabbed his hand back, and they had a firm handshake.

"Ree-On? Like Ryan, but fancier?" Nick asked.

Rion smiled. "That's the first time someone described it like that. But yeah, I guess so."

He nodded, then said his name repeatedly. "Rion. Reee-on. I like it. Rion." Red shirt, now named Nick, smiled to himself. "Does it mean anything?"

"Yes. It means king."

Nick looked skeptical. "You're shitting me."

"I shit you not. It's Gaelic for king. Apparently, I was named after my father."

"Was? I'm sorry if he passed."

Rion shrugged. "I have no idea if he did or didn't."

"Oh. Never met him?"

Rion scoffed. "He never met me."

Nick nodded. "Cute and cocky. I like it." Rion felt himself blushing, so he quickly turned away. "Business or pleasure?" Nick asked.

Rion turned back to Nick. "Both. I'm a writer. I'm working on a novel, so I'm doing some research, but also pleasure because I've never been to Europe before."

"Nice," he responded.

"And you? Business or pleasure?" Rion turned the question back to him.

"Business. I come at least once a year to meet with my investor."

"Ah. I could tell by your shoes."

Nick looked down at his Tom Ford leather cap-toe shoes and smiled. "My shoes?"

"That you have money," Rion said definitively. "Or make money. Lots of it."

He nodded. "And what do your blue and white retro air Jordans say about you?"

Rion looked down and smiled. "How did you know they were retro Jordans?"

Nick laughed. "You must really take me for a rich, pretty-boy, huh?"

"Who said you were pretty?" Rion grimaced at him, making Nick laugh out loud again.

They felt the plane begin to move as the lights dimmed, catching Rion off guard. He gasped and looked straight ahead. Nick noticed but didn't make a comment. He could tell Rion was scared. Rion closed his eyes and counted backward from fifty until the plane settled in the air. Then he turned the overhead light on and continued to write in his notebook.

Rion stretched out on the seat next to him and outlined the beginning chapters of his story. Nick pulled out his laptop and went over his numbers again, then read through a couple of editorials sent to him for final approval. The flight attendant came around and offered soda and water, and they both took a coke with an extra glass of ice. Nick looked at Rion when he got the same.

Rion answered his silent question. "I like to chew on ice. It calms my anxiety about flying."

"You don't fly often?" Nick asked.

"It's my first time on a plane," Rion admitted.

"Oh wow. You're popping your cherry right now," Nick said, amused. "Glad to be a part of it."

Rion chuckled. "Is that why you get extra ice?"

Nick shook his head. "I'm always flying. I just like to have extra ice. They never give you enough."

Rion nodded back. "So what kind of work do you do that you need an investor?" Rion asked, forgetting his vow not to start a conversation with another stranger on the plane.

Nick answered, "I run a magazine. It used to be fully paper, but we moved online about three years ago to reach a wider audience. My meeting in two days is to decide if we want to scrap the physical copies of the magazine and continue to work online only instead."

"Wow. What's your magazine? Maybe I've heard of it."

Nick hesitated, then told him, "Deep Strokez."

Rion doubled-blinked. "Deep. Strokes."

Nick laughed. "Look it up now. The last 's' is a 'z.'"

Rion was already hooked onto the airplane Wi-Fi and put in the URL. What popped up was *Deep Strokez: The first and last stop for all sex-related news.*

"Holy, holy shit!" Rion said loudly, then covered his mouth as passengers turned to look at him.

Nick smiled, then shrugged. "It's a job."

"It's a lifestyle," Rion said with a laugh. "How long have you been running it?"

"I started it as a gag in college with my roommate when I was nineteen years old. We wrote our own underground paper on sex-related news on campus. I was a journalism major, and he was a communications major, so we had all the resources we needed to do it. We kept it going all throughout college and then turned it into an actual magazine when we graduated. Three years ago, he decided he didn't want to do it anymore and started doing other journalist work, so I took on an investor, and we changed it to an online platform."

"Wow. Do you write articles, too?" Rion asked as he continued to scroll through the magazine.

"No, not anymore. I have sixteen main reporters for all the various parts of sex-related news, from actual real-life sex stories to celebrity news, educational articles, LGBTQ news, and an advice column. We also hire freelance writers here and there if you're interested. I did hear you say you're a writer."

"That's ... really nice of you to offer. Thanks. But you don't even know if my stuff is good."

"I have a good feeling about you, Rion. Call it intuition."

Nick reached into his pocket and pulled out a shiny white card with gold lettering. Rion read: *Nicholas*

*E. Highton, CEO, Managing Editor. Deep Strokez Publication.* The address, phone number, and personal email were on it. Rion slid it into his bag. He put a mini blanket over his jeans and put his pillow behind his head.

"So, what kind of writing do you do?" Nick asked, also getting comfortable, leaning his seat all the way back.

It was Rion's turn to hesitate. "Fiction. Contemporary Romance. Family Dramas. Things like that."

"Cool. Are you published?"

"Yeah, actually. I have a three-book contract with my publisher, and two have been published already. The third one is scheduled to come out next year."

"So you're an author, not just a writer," Nick confirmed with a nod.

Rion smiled, surprised at the warm spot that was forming in his chest at Nick's words. "Yeah. I'm an author. I'm working on my fourth book now. The manuscript is due in six months. I'm using the advance from it to finance this trip."

"Sounds good. Anything I've read before?"

"Probably not your genre," Rion said with a sly smirk.

"What, not sexy enough?" Nick smiled back at him.

Rion didn't answer. He turned away thinking, *if only he knew.*

They continued talking in low voices about nothing important as the food cart finally made it to them. Nick chose the Salisbury steak, while Rion chose the chicken, thinking it would be a safe choice. But he was thoroughly disappointed. After a couple of bites, he opted to eat the bread dipped in applesauce instead.

Nick looked over and laughed. "You mean airplane chicken smothered in questionable brown sauce didn't do it for you?"

Rion cringed. "Not my idea of a good time." Nick laughed loudly at that, making Rion chuckle as heads turned again. "You're going to get us kicked off the plane. We're literally the only ones talking. Everyone else is trying to sleep."

"Should I move closer so you can hear me?" Nick asked.

"Only if you let me keep my legs across your lap," Rion said jokingly. "And also, your applesauce as payment, sir."

"I'll do you one better." Nick stood up and opened the compartment, rummaging around the front pocket of his carry-on. He pulled out a large bag of Cool Ranch Doritos. "Never leave home without them."

"Dude, score!" Rion whispered excitedly.

Nick came over, and Rion put his feet down, but as soon as Nick sat down next to him, he stretched back over his thighs. Nick casually put his arms across Rion's legs as Rion opened the bag of chips, took a bite.

He sighed. "So good. So, so good. Especially after a bud or edibles."

Nick was surprised. "I wouldn't have taken you for a weed smoker."

Rion shrugged. "I'm an artist. What can I say?" Nick chuckled. "Honestly, I don't do it often. Only when my anxiety is really high, and I just need something to bring it back down. I have a medicinal card, not that I need it anymore since it's legal recreationally."

Nick smiled and squeezed his leg. "Good old California. New York is next."

Rion held the bag out to him, and they ate together as they continued talking. Nick shared how he came from a family of overachievers that acted like they were the new millennium's Rockefeller Family, buying up land and businesses and selling them for parts. "My older sister Emma is a high-powered corporate attorney and works in the family business, my older brother Brian is a world-renowned spinal surgeon, and I own a sex mag. Can you tell who's the black sheep of the family? Even though I'm the one with the lightest hair color."

"So you're the baby in your family at twenty-six?"

"Twenty-seven," Nick corrected. "Yesterday was my birthday, May 30th. And yeah, I'm the baby of the family," Nick stated.

"Happy birthday, Nick," Rion said with a smile. "I'm the baby of my family, too. At twenty-five."

Rion told Nick about his family, namely about his three older sisters, who were all underachievers, showing him his tattoo of their initials, M. A. G., going down his left arm. "Roslyn, the woman who gave me life, is a recovering crack-cocaine addict. Not sure how long this recession from drugs is going to last this time. Muriel has three children by three different fathers, taking up after her mother, and is a full-time waitress. Avalon, Ava, dropped out of school to get her GED and join the police force, only to be kicked out of there for her bi-polar disorder and is now bouncing around a couple of odd jobs. Last I checked, she was a bouncer at a strip club. Gabby, she tried, though. She tried really hard to break the cycle. She finished high school and started college but got pregnant and dropped out. She works for the post office and is a single mom. I love my six year old niece, Morgan. I'm her second parent. She gives all of us hope that the children of Roslyn will make something of themselves one day."

"Sounds like you broke the cycle, though," Nick said.

"Yeah, I did. Graduated high school. Got an Associate's degree. Published author. Financially able to take care of my sisters now. I'm proud of myself. I'm pretty great," Rion said smugly.

"So the baby of the family is who everyone looks up to. That's a lot of pressure to keep being great."

Rion's smile faded a bit. "Yeah. Yeah, it is."

Nick said, "My therapist reminds me that it's not up to me to carry the achievements of the Hightons. It's up to me to motivate myself and achieve the things that I want. My rise and fall does not reflect on my entire family's legacy. I'm just one person. Just me."

Rion smirked. "I wish it were that simple. But I guess it is for you."

Nick grimaced. "What does that mean?"

"C'mon. The new millennium's Rockefellers? That sounds like your family is rolling in money. If you rise or fall, no one else in your family is going to be affected. But if I fall, who pays for my mother's apartment or her rehab when she hits rock bottom again, or makes sure Morgan has childcare so Gabby can get to work? You and me, we are not the same."

Nick took in his words. "Maybe not. But I know what it feels like not to live up to your own expectations. The pressure not to fail. The burning urge to not say fuck it and run away. Daily. Waking up in the middle of the night with your chest closing up because you're this close to losing it all. I just meant I get it."

Rion nodded. "Yeah. You should smoke more bud."

Nick laughed out loud, and Rion giggled until it turned into a yawn. "Uh-oh. Somebody wants to go nighty-night," Nick said.

"What time is it?" Rion asked with another yawn and adjusted the small pillow behind him.

"In America or in England?" Nick asked. Rion closed his eyes and smiled. Nick looked at his watch. "4:34 in New York. 9:34 a.m. where we're going."

Rion nodded with his eyes closed. Nick stared at him, taking in his curly dark brown hair, thick eyebrows, thin mustache, and even thinner goatee. He watched Rion's breathing slow down and knew he had fallen asleep. Nick had the strongest urge to reach out and touch his face, trace his pink lips with the pad of his finger. Instead, he leaned his chair all the way back and closed his eyes as well.

Two hours later, they were both woken up by the cart bringing breakfast. Rion took his legs off Nick, and they simultaneously lowered their trays down to accept their food.

"So, where are you staying?" Nick asked between bites.

Rion shrugged. "No clue," he replied with food in his mouth. He swallowed, then said, "I was just going to take a cab over to Brixton and find a place there."

Nick's eyes bugged out of his head. "Brixton? What's your story about? A white American willingly getting mugged looking for weed in South London?"

Rion spit out food in laughter. "Not quite. But close."

"So you just ... jumped on a plane for the first time to a country you've never been to with no place to lay your head tonight?" Nick was in awe.

"Yup. But I'll always find a place to lay my head," Rion said nonchalantly. "The perks of being home-less at various stages in my life, once again, thanks to Roslyn."

"Wow," was all Nick could say.

"Yup." Rion shrugged again and changed the sub-ject. "This breakfast is way better than dinner. They should stick to that."

Nick chuckled and handed him his morning bis-cuit. "I'm not a big carb guy, except for Doritos. More protein and veggies."

"Okay, Popeye," Rion joked and happily took his biscuit, reaching over for his butter, too.

By the time they were done eating, cleared, and had raised their trays, the announcement came on. "Good morning, passengers. We will be landing at Heathrow in forty-five minutes. Please take a minute to look around for any last items and trash and gather your belongings before the seatbelt light comes on."

They stood up and stretched, then picked up the empty Doritos bag, candy wrappers, and small plastic cups.

"Guess I should move back to my seat," Nick said casually.

"See you across the pond," Rion responded.

Nick smiled at him, then moved over to his original seat. He repacked his laptop bag and sat down. Rion busied himself with a game on his cell phone. Both tried not to turn back to the other while the plane was landing. Rion slid a piece of gum into his mouth and closed his eyes. He began to count backward and calm his nerves. Nick looked over at him, and at the last minute, got up and switched seats before the flight attendant saw him.

Rion opened his eyes in surprise as Nick plopped down and clicked his seatbelt. "You look like you're going to throw up. Thought you might like some company," Nick said nonchalantly.

Rion opened his mouth slightly as they stared at each other. The plane lurched down and he instinctively grabbed Nick's wrist. He faced forward, closed his eyes again, and remembered to breathe.

Nick slid his hand back to hold Rion's hand, and Rion did not pull away. Instead, he grabbed his hand tighter. Every time the plane lunged farther down, Rion squeezed.

"I hate this," he murmured. "Why did I do this again?"

"Because you're writing the great American novel, and to do that, you need to go beyond your comfort zone," Nick responded. Rion smiled without looking at him.

The plane landed with a big jolt, making Rion yelp. Nick squeezed his hand again, then patted it with his other hand. Rion finally turned to him. "Thanks, Nicky."

Nick grimaced at him. "Dude. I am Nicholas or Nick. Never Nicky." He shook his head.

Rion laughed. "Sure thing, Nicky." Nick squeezed his hand tighter. "Ah! Okay, okay, Nick. Got it."

Nick eased up but didn't let go just yet. They stared at each other with smiles on their faces as other passengers rose around them to gather their belongings. Rion flexed his hand, and Nick finally let him go, turning away first.

"Yeah. Sorry," Nick mumbled. He stood up and grabbed his bag from the compartment.

Rion waited until he was done and took his orange bookbag down as well. They continued to stare at each other, then glanced away as they waited for their turn to get off the plane. Nick gestured for Rion to go first, and he did. They walked off the plane together in silence and then stopped at the gate.

Nick spoke first. "It was really great meeting you, Rion. I hope not for the last time. I meant it when I said call me if you ever want to write for me."

"Thanks. I just might when I get back."

They moved closer and awkwardly shook hands. Then Rion turned around and went through the gate for baggage claim. Nick watched him for a moment, then turned in the opposite direction, stopping on the ground floor at Starbucks. He stood in a long line to get his mocha latte grande and tried not to think about the stranger he had just met on a plane.

*R*ion waited at the carousel for his bright orange suitcase with the small rainbow sticker on the handle. Once he retrieved his bag, he made his way outside to the long taxi line. He yawned a bit and looked around, then saw Nick's red shirt eight people in front of him, with his face buried in his phone.

"Sup, Nicky!" he called out playfully.

Nick lifted his head and paused, then slowly turned around to see Rion's smiling face. "We have got to stop meeting like this," Nick said.

Rion laughed. Nick gave him a wide smile and moved up the line. Rion called Gabby to let her know he was okay, then started a game on his phone, trying really hard not to look at Nicholas again.

When it was Nick's turn to get a cab, he waited patiently until one drove up. He put his bag in the trunk and opened the passenger door. But then he got an idea. "Hey, Ree. Need a lift?"

Rion looked up from his phone. "Ree? Really?" The only people that called him "Ree" were his family.

"If I'm Nicky, then you're Ree," said Nick.

"But Nicky is so much cuter," Rion teased.

"Do you want a ride or not?" Nick said, narrowing his eyes at him.

"I always want to ride," Rion said before he could stop himself, then blushed bashfully. Nick smiled, unsure if it was double meaning. Rion stepped out of the line and brought his suitcase over to the trunk, and put it in. He slid into the car beside Nick and put his bookbag in his lap.

"Address, sirs?" the cabby asked.

"Erm..." Rion started.

"The Mandarin Oriental, Hyde Park," Nick answered. The car pulled off.

Rion looked at him, about to ask a question, but Nick spoke first. "Listen. I know you have this huge plan to visit the slums of England, but for the next six days, at least have a decent place to lay your head. I have a two-bedroom suite, and you can crash in the other room. What do you say?"

Rion was thoughtful. As much as he would love to be in a luxury hotel, at least for one night, he wanted to make sure Nick was clear about what he was asking.

"So I think I should tell you something before I agree to this."

Nick scrunched up his face. "Are you a serial killer?"

"Worse," Rion said seriously. "I'm gay. Very gay."

Nick did not flinch. "Okay. I would have never guessed."

"Most people don't know unless I tell them."

"And you're telling me because...?"

"I just..." Rion hesitated. "I thought you should know. Before you offer up a room in your suite to me."

Nick smiled. "Should I be worried about you pouncing on me in the middle of the night? Since you always want to *ride*?"

Rion laughed and blushed again. "No. I mean... you're attractive and all. But... no. That's not... not what I'm here for."

"Hmmm... Too bad," Nick said with a straight face, making Rion blush a third time. He turned away quickly to look out the window. They were quiet for a moment, and then Nick asked in a low voice, "Just for clarification, when you say, 'very gay'..."

Rion turned back and looked him right in the eye. "Very gay. Very, very gay." He pulled up the sleeve on his right forearm and showed Nick his other tattoo, a fountain pen that was dripping ink, each drop a color of the rainbow.

"Aha. Good to know." Nick let a moment pass, then reached out and trailed one finger down the length of the pen on his skin. He said, "So I've been known to ... explore here and there with my own ... kind."

Rion chuckled a little nervously as his body below reacted to Nick's touch. "Okay. A little exploration is ... a good thing." He slid his sweater sleeve down.

They turned their heads away from one another and were quiet again. Then Nick asked softly, "So... Would you follow a complete stranger to a hotel room and ... explore with him?"

Rion chose his words very carefully. "I've been known to explore with strangers before."

Nick nodded. "Well. I've been known to invite strangers into my hotel room before."

Rion turned to him again. "Is that why you invited me to stay?"

"No!" Nick said automatically and turned to Rion, shaking his head for emphasis. "I invited you to stay with me before I knew, didn't I?"

"You could have assumed—"

Nick cut him off. "I didn't. I honestly was just inviting a new and interesting friend with nowhere to go to have a place to lay his head for the next couple of nights while I'm in town. That's it. No expectations or preconceived notions."

Rion was quietly thinking. He liked Nick. Nick was smart, quick-witted, and sexy. And he hadn't been laid in a while, so it wouldn't be the worst thing in the world. In fact, it might be just what he needed to finally get Jason, his ex, out from under his skin. But in order to not look too eager, he said cautiously, "Well, let's just see how the week goes instead of making plans. Maybe you will get your wish. Or maybe I just need a place to sleep after eleven hours on a long plane ride."

"Absolutely," Nick said. "No pressure. Just a place to lay your head. Anything else would be completely up to you."

"Thanks. I appreciate that, Nick."

"Sure, Ree." Rion smiled at Nick, and Nick smiled back.

When they arrived, Nick went to the front desk and checked in, then turned around and handed Rion a key card. "So you can come and go as you please. You're not beholden to me."

"Thanks," Rion said softly. He followed Nick to the elevator and then to the penthouse suite. Upon entrance, his mouth dropped open. "Holy, holy shit."

The room was contemporarily designed, with an open floor plan of a living room, dining room, and kitchen area. A long sectional faced a TV mounted over a fireplace. A terrace decorated with simple floral arrangements had views directly into Hyde Park. Nick walked to the right into the hallway and opened the master bedroom. Rion followed, still unable to close his mouth. The bedroom had very little furniture but was amazingly elegant. A king-sized bed faced a wall of windows that opened into another terrace with a table on it.

Nick dropped his bag and turned around to smile at Rion. "My room. Yours is this way." He led Rion back out to another room along the hallway that had two queen-sized beds. "Pick any one you want."

Rion smiled, dropped his suitcase, and flopped on the nearest bed. The softness of the mattress was enough to make him happy. "I can't believe you live like this every day."

"Not exactly. Maybe one day you'll see my apartment."

Rion looked up at him. Nick smiled and turned around. "I'll leave you to it. I'm going to take a shower and get some work done in the living room. Rest, and we'll catch up for dinner, yes?"

"Yes," Rion replied. As Nick was closing the door, Rion said, "Thanks again, Nicky."

Nick turned around to see his smile. The smile he was beginning to want to see all the time. "Nick," he reminded him and gently closed the door.

Rion laid back down. He thought he would be sleepy and jet-lagged, but instead, he felt energized. And horny. He had been keeping sexual thoughts out of his mind the entire trip until Nick's confession in the cab about his exploration with men. He wanted to know what level of exploration he had done before. He wanted to know how big his penis was and if he could wrap his hand around it. Or better, if he could deep-throat it. Or take all of him inside and ride it. He wanted to know what his lips tasted like. What his sweat tasted like. He wanted the stranger named Nicholas Highton, badly.

After ruminating on his sexual fantasies, he decided to take a shower. Rion opened the door to his room to cross the hall to the bathroom. He heard the shower going in the master bedroom since Nick left his room door open. Rion sighed and went into the spacious bathroom. He entered the shower and stood under the water. He kept imagining Nick's body, wondering if he had hair on his torso, hair on his genitals.

"Shit," he said to himself. If it was this bad, and it was barely day one, how was he going to make it through the next five days? If he thought Nick was completely straight, he wouldn't even be entertaining this idea. Why did Nick tell him he wasn't? Did he want Rion as badly as Rion wanted him?

Rion adjusted the water to lukewarm and cooled his body off. He quickly showered and opened the bathroom door with the towel around his waist. Nick happened to be walking by and jumped back.

"Oh! Sorry," Rion said first.

"Don't be. I'm enjoying the view," Nick said seductively and winked.

But he continued on down the hall to the living room, leaving Rion in shambles. Nick had changed into a pair of tan linen pants and a white t-shirt, and Rion was sure he was not wearing underwear as he watched his muscled ass walk away from him. Rion's cock twitched. He quickly went into the room and closed the door.

He laid on the bed and started touching himself over the towel, then removed it and grabbed his manhood. It was already hard in his hands, leaking pre-cum. "God, why am I torturing myself like this?" he asked himself out loud.

*Because you don't want to act like a flighty slut*, he answered himself in his head.

After going back and forth, he said to himself, "Fuck it," and stood up. He put on a tank top and a pair of sweatpants, and grabbed supplies to put in his pocket. He walked out of the room and went into the living room, where Nick was sitting on the sofa with his feet crossed at the ankles on the glass coffee table, laptop on his lap, tapping away, biting his bottom lip.

Rion came over and sat at the other end of the couch. Nick kept typing but asked, "You okay?"

"Yeah. Yeah, I'm ... okay."

"You hungry yet?

"No."

Nick nodded. He paused typing, then glanced at Rion. "What?"

"Nothing," Rion replied softly. Nick nodded again. He looked back down at his laptop and continued working. Rion sighed and said, "I don't ... do this."

"Do what?" Nick asked without looking up.

"This ... thing I'm about to do."

Nick stopped typing and looked at him again. Rion stared back, then stood up. He walked over to Nick as Nick folded his laptop. Rion stepped over his legs and straddled them, standing up. Nick looked up at him, then put his feet down and his laptop to the side. Rion reached inside his sweatpants and stroked himself. Nick opened his legs wider, sliding to the edge of the couch, and Rion walked into them, not breaking eye contact. Nick slowly reached up and caressed Rion's thighs and around to his bottom, then squeezed them both at the same time.

"Take it out," Nick said softly.

Rion did, his seven and a half inches aching in his hand, the head soaked in pre-cum. Nick took it from him. Rion's eyes fluttered as Nick's strong hands wrapped around his cock, and he watched Nick's lips wrap around his cock head, licking the cum. Rion moaned and ran his fingers through the top of Nick's hair, encouraging him. Nick took the hint and slid the rest of Rion's cock down his throat until his balls were tucked under Nick's chin, then he slowly slid up to the head, keeping his eyes on Rion. Nick hummed on his way down and back up a few more times, enforcing that Rion had made the right decision.

Rion pulled out of Nick's mouth and stepped back. He dropped to his knees and tugged at the sides of Nick's house pants. Nick lifted up just enough for Rion to pull his pants down, and his cock flopped back against his stomach. Nick instinctively grabbed it and stroked, but Rion took it from him and quickly slid his lips over the head and down halfway, greedily sucking his larger-than-expected cock.

"Fuuuck," Nick groaned and held onto Rion's curls with both hands, guiding his bob.

Every time Rion came up, Nick quickly pushed his head back down and thrust up at the same time. To Rion's credit, he did not gag on Nick's nine inches; he took it down his throat like a pro, sucking in his cheeks on the way up. Nick let him continue until he had to make him stop.

"What do you have on you?" he asked breathlessly.

Rion slowed down but did not stop sucking Nick's cock, as he put his hands in his pocket and took out the miniature bottle of KY Warming Liquid and a condom. He placed it on the couch next to Nick's thigh and continued to swallow his pre-cum.

Nick moaned and told him, "Stand up and turn around."

Rion quickly obliged. He stood up and pulled down his pants. He bent over and placed two hands on the glass coffee table. Nick placed the condom on first, then slid to the edge of the couch, spread Rion's cheeks, and put his tongue right into the hole.

"God!" Rion yelled and shivered.

Nick did not stop, first putting a bite mark on Rion's left cheek. He aggressively licked, sucked, spit, and slurped up Rion's entire anus for a few minutes before he decided to stop torturing them both and added the lubricant to his fingers. He fingered Rion with two, then three fingers before he stood up, took off his shirt, and pulled up Rion's tank top, exposing his long but arched back. He licked his lips and kissed the back of Rion's neck, making him moan some more before he lined up his cock and gently inserted it inside of Rion.

Rion gasped, then relaxed and let him in. Nick made a couple of shallow pumps, holding onto his waist, pushing in deeper and deeper with every thrust until he slid past his prostate to the hilt. Rion let out a satisfied moan. Nick paused, then began to move faster.

"Fuck, yeah," Nick murmured as he slammed into Rion over and over again.

"Fuuuck ... meeee..." Rion moaned. He leaned over even more on one elbow, taking Nick with him, so he could grab onto his own leaking cock and begin to tug on it.

Nick found his rhythm again and thrust. They both felt the climax growing in their bodies. It hit Rion first, the rub against his internal bundle of nerves maximizing his pleasure. He let out a soft, "Aaaah," and ropes of cum shot out onto the glass table. Nick came right behind him in the condom.

Nick pulled out and fell backward onto the couch, saying, "Holy shit, that was awesome."

Rion knelt first, then sat back against the couch between Nick's legs. He closed his eyes and tried to catch his breath. He felt Nick's hand in his curls, massaging his scalp softly, sweetly. It made him smile.

"Are you okay?" Nick asked softly.

"Uh-hmm..." Rion replied.

"Okay. Because that was incredible. And I wouldn't mind doing it again if ... you're okay with that?"

Rion turned all the way around and rose onto his knees to face him. He put both hands on Nick's thighs. They stayed that way for another moment, then Nick gently took Rion's face in his hands. He moved his face quickly toward him, but then paused right before their lips touched. Rion moved in the last centimeter and touched his lips to Nick's soft ones. Their lips continued to press against each other, pull back, then press again, both hesitant about the level of intimacy they were having, although they were sexually intimate moments ago. And yet, it felt so natural. Rion somehow knew Nick would not do it first, so he took the chance and opened his mouth slightly to pull Nick's lips into his own.

Nick opened his mouth, and Rion stuck his tongue inside. Nick moaned and allowed Rion to kiss him like they were old lovers, not strangers who had met on a plane twelve hours earlier. But Rion liked everything about Nick, he discovered at that moment. He liked how handsome and laid back he was. He liked his personality. He liked fucking him. And the icing on the cake was how much he liked kissing him. He wanted Nick to stay in his life he decided. But for how long would be the question.

Rion gently pulled out of the kiss first, one that left Nick visibly excited as his breathing was labored and his cock was hard again.

"Your room or mine?" Rion asked.

*N*icholas was deep inside of Rion for the third time and couldn't believe how unbelievable it felt. Everything about it looked, smelled, and felt right to him. Rion's legs were up and bent to the sides of him as Nick plowed him at a steady pace. His curls were matted to his forehead in sweat, his face pink and flushed. His eyes were squeezed tightly shut, and his wide pink lips were slightly opened as he moaned. His fingers were wrapped around Nick's biceps, squeezing so tightly that his fingertips and nails were white. Every couple of minutes, Nick had to lean over and kiss Rion's lips, run his hands through his damp hair, and reassure Rion that he was right there with him.

It wasn't supposed to happen like this for him. Nick technically had someone, albeit a boring someone, that his mother continued to push on him. He struck up a conversation with the man with curly brown hair and wide brown eyes to be polite. Then he continued talking to him because he was interesting. He thought, at most, he would get a good friend, possibly a free-lance employee, out of it, since he had said he was a writer. He offered his hotel room as a good gesture for a new friend. But once Rion turned to him with his pretty brown eyes and full lips and said the words, "I'm gay," something clicked in his brain. His immediate reaction was to pull his face close and stick his tongue down Rion's throat. Because the reaction was so strong, he did the complete opposite and didn't give a reaction at all. Instead, he casually let him know that he was open sexually and that if he wanted something more than a bed to lay his head in at night, he would be around.

But he couldn't stop thinking about it for the rest of the cab ride to the hotel. On the elevator ride up to the penthouse, he was staring at Rion's beautiful features, wondering what his mouth tasted like, what his cock tasted like. Taking his shower, he almost jerked off, something Nick didn't do often. But when Rion opened the door in his towel with his pale skin with curly brown chest hair in various spots stuck to his body, his abs beautifully crafted down to the V at his groin, his pen tattoo on his right forearm with ink drops in rainbow colors, he couldn't help but make a seductive comment. Who knew that would be the catalyst that would propel Rion to come out of his room and approach him? Nick had finally pushed the beautiful man out of his head, focusing on adding notes to his PowerPoint, and there Rion was, with desire written all over him, nervousness in his eyes at "what he was about to do." He needed permission to give in to his desire. And Nicholas gave it to him, gave it to them both.

But even still, it was supposed to be a fun fuck. The first time, banging his back out over the coffee table, was. The second time he brought Rion into his bed, and Rion immediately went face down, ass up for him. Nick loved how eager a bottom he was and happily obliged, lasting longer the second time, quickly figuring out what angle Rion liked the most, the one that put the most pressure on his prostate until they both came again.

Afterward, Rion said breathlessly, "Now I'm hungry."

Nick asked, "Want a burger? They make great burgers here."

Rion laughed. "How did you know I like burgers?"

"Call it intuition," Nick said with a smile.

"Yeah, but it has to be like a Whopper-level burger for me to like it," Rion said seriously.

Nicholas couldn't help but laugh. "If Burger King is your gold standard of burgers, you've been missing out."

"Don't knock a Whopper with cheese, rich boy," Rion teased, making Nick laugh again.

He ordered room service, and they ate cheeseburgers and fries on his bed, mostly in silence, which was a stark contrast with how much they had talked on the plane. Right afterward, Rion fell backward onto the pillow and quickly fell asleep, his body and belly satisfied. Nick had moved the trays aside and found himself lying next to him, watching him sleep until he too fell into slumber.

Rion woke him up hours later with kisses on his face, his arms, and the large labyrinth tattoo spread across his right shoulder and back. The sun had gone down completely, and the only light was the soft glow of the bulbs on the terrace. Nick opened his eyes and looked up at Rion's precious and beautiful face. He put his lips on Rion's chin and the sides of his mouth, teasing him before he pulled his top lip between his. Their passion for each other was undeniable at that point, their tongues perfectly massaging each other. He didn't know how long they had kissed, but he knew he didn't want to stop. The only thing that made it end was Rion, who pulled out another condom from somewhere and pressed it against his chest during their kiss.

Nick looked down, then back up into Rion's expectant eyes. Rion moved backward and laid down face up. They hadn't done it face up yet. It seemed too personal, too real. And yet, it was all he wanted to do. He slid the condom on, felt around for Rion's hole, and found it already silky wet. He growled at him, making Rion smile slyly. But he still took his time and entered him slowly, starting out with Rion's legs against his chest, his feet on his shoulders. Rion held his hands straight out as if surrendering to the pleasure and pain, and grabbed the sheets with every thrust. It meant everything to Nick.

He had to get closer. He took Rion's legs off his torso and leaned over him, and Rion wrapped his legs around his back. Rion moved his hands, running them through Nick's chest hair, then landed on his biceps. And there they stayed as Nick inadvertently made love to the stranger from the plane.

Rion slid his hands between them and grabbed hold of his cock again, stroking gently. Nick rotated his hips and grinded against him and gave him what he wanted, what he needed to cum. Rion's body tensed against him as strands of cum painted his chest, then he sighed, whispering his name, "Nicky."

Nick hated being called "Nicky." He shed his nickname as early as twelve years old, stopping all his family members from calling him Baby Nicky. He was already the youngest of his family, the youngest of his cousins, and the smallest until he shot up at fifteen and kept growing to a strong 6'4". He was always Nick and never Nicky. But, at that moment, hearing Rion call his name like that, his heart exploded, and the name had never felt sweeter. He was never Nicky, except to Rion, he would always be Nicky.

He began to move faster, burying deeper, needing to feel all of him. Rion cried out, and Nick exploded for the third time into a condom. He slid out and put his face on Rion's chest, only then remembering he had cum there as it stuck to his ear and hair. He didn't mind, though, and Rion didn't either. This third time around, it was something more emotional, more connecting. They both felt it, but neither of them spoke about it. Instead, they watched the sunrise in London, although it was still in the middle of the night for them, and fell back asleep.

Nick woke a few hours later with the sunlight in his eyes, still lying on Rion's chest. He moved away from him, and Rion turned over in his sleep. He bent down and kissed Rion's face gently so as not to wake him before he went to take a shower. He was to meet Parker at his office first at 3 p.m. to go over his presentation for tomorrow, then do their customary drinks and catch up.

Parker was one of his best friends from Harvard. He came over as an exchange student from Oxford for just a semester, but they quickly became friends and kept in touch over the years. When Nicholas had casually mentioned that Lionel wanted to be bought out of the magazine, Parker unexpectedly stepped up, offering to invest in the magazine through his advertising company. He just had to prove to his board that the investment was worth it, and he had every year for the last two years. He wasn't really nervous about it, but this year he was making a huge change, going completely online, and he wasn't sure what the board would say about it. But work was the last thing on Nick's mind as he took his shower. He took his time, remembering Rion calling his name in the middle of the night. He didn't know what was happening between them, but he knew he had to keep Rion in his life somehow.

He came out of the bathroom, and Rion was still sound asleep. He got dressed quietly and looked at the time: 2:30 p.m. He had to get going.

"Ree," he called his name softly as he stood above him.

"Hmmm," Rion responded without moving or opening up his eyes.

"I have to go."

Rion sighed, then turned over to look up at Nick, his eyes still lidded. "I don't know what time I'll be back. You'll be okay on your own, right?" Nick asked.

"Um-hmm," he replied.

"Order room service for breakfast, whatever you want."

"Um-hmm."

Nick couldn't help it. Rion was such a cutie. He leaned over and kissed his lips. He tried to pull back, but Rion reached up and held his neck to push their lips together again. He moved to Nick's neck and began kissing him there.

"Hmm... I really want to get back in this bed with you, but I really have to go."

Rion reluctantly let go of his neck and Nick rose to a stand, his cock straining in his Armani suit. "I'll be fine," Rion told him. "I'm going to step out soon and find a cab to head to Brixton for a while. Don't worry about me."

"Just be safe and smart," Nick told him in a fatherly fashion.

"I will be," Rion reassured him. "Good luck meeting with your investor today."

"Thanks." He bent down once more for a peck and then turned around before he stayed a minute longer.

The taxi stopped ten minutes later in front of the building that said *Parker Madison, Inc* on it. He straightened out his tie and entered through the revolving doors, stopping at the huge front desk. "Nicholas Highton for Parker Madison."

"Of course, Mr. Highton. How are you today?" the ice-blonde-haired receptionist asked him as she picked up her phone. "Please let Mr. Madison know that Mr. Highton is here." She hung up and handed him a blue badge. "This will get you in the far left elevator."

Nick knew exactly where his friend's office was, but smiled a thank you at her, anyway. He made his way to Parker's office and passed his personal assistant,

Jamila. She nodded at him and continued typing. Nick could hear Parker already yelling at someone when he opened the wooden door and closed it behind him.

"—to think for a second that it's what I want. What the bloody fuck are you on, mate!? No... no... NOOO, are you listening!? Stop talking, you fucktard and listen! It's not a deal I would take if you promised a knob slob by Princess Kate herself. Fix it. NOW!"

Parker pressed his headset and pulled it off his head. He looked at Nick and said, "I miss the days of slamming the phone down on an arsehole." Nick took his laptop bag off his shoulder and met Parker in the middle of his expansive office for a hug. "How are you, mate?"

"Great. Really, really great," Nick replied. "And I see you're still making people taller than you feel small."

Parker patted his shoulder. "Only small people feel small around me. You never did."

"That's because I'm bigger than you. Literally," Nick teased. Parker was 5'7" with a good pair of heels.

"Fuck off," Parker said with a smile. "Now, let's see these numbers."

They moved over to the table and Nick opened up his laptop, connecting it to the projector, and they got to work. Three hours later, Parker had given Nick pointers on his speech to the board members and encouraged his projections. "I'm behind this one hundred percent. Now let's get plastered, yes? Off to Julie's then."

Parker called the car around, and they moved on to dinner at Julie's Restaurant and Champagne Bar, discussing work at first, then their individual family gossip. They ended dinner with an order of cognac, and a different waitress came over to deliver them, bending over to show her cleavage before lifting up and saying, "Anything else I can do for you gentlemen?"

Parker looked up at her and said, "Oh, I can think of plenty you can do for me. But for now, the drinks are enough."

She smiled at him, but looked over longingly at Nick. Nick gave her a small smile and turned away. Her smile turned down, and she walked away disappointed.

"Whoa, mate. I think she wanted to end up in your bed tonight," Parker said, and took a sip. "Why the snub?"

Nick took a sip and said, "My bed is currently occupied."

Parker grimaced. "Not bloody Penny again!" Nick was about to deny it when Parker continued to rant. "Ugh. I told you to drop this a year ago. Falling into the pressures of dear old mum convincing you that you should be married by now. Well, I've warned you before, and I'll warn you again, do not marry that one. She's a bore now, she'll become an insufferable bore as a wife. You don't love her, you don't even really like her, and you'll regret having children with her. She's just after your family money and your clout, and you know it." He took a bigger gulp of his Villon.

"Not Penny," Nick said simply and sipped.

Parker smiled widely. "You dirty dog you!" Nick chuckled as Parker reached out and playfully shoved his shoulder. "Well, come on, spill. What stray did you pick up between yesterday and today? And please, for God's sake, Nick, describe her nipples to me exactly.

I know you're not a tits man, but I am, and that's the least you could do for me." Parker waited expectedly.

Nick took another small sip and said, "His name is Rion."

Both of Parker's eyebrows went up. "*He*, you say? It's been a long time since I heard that pronoun come from your lips in a sexual nature. Now I really want to know all the details."

He stretched his feet across to the other side of the booth. Nick slouched and did the same, and confessed all about meeting Rion on the plane and that there was an instant connection leading to an intense sexual attraction. Parker listened without commentary, which Nick appreciated, until the end.

"So, I don't know. I don't know if this is just a vacation thing. I could get back to my hotel, and he could be completely gone. I just realized I don't even have his cell number. But I know there is something about him that I just… It's too magnetic. I want him in my life. This could go nowhere. Or it could go everywhere. I just don't know."

"Bloody hell, mate," Parker started. "You surely have got yourself balls-up here. Let's think about this logically, shall we?"

"Let's," Nick agreed. "I think I need some level-headed advice."

"You and Rion are from completely different worlds. He just recently crawled himself out from below the poverty line, and you are practically a Kennedy." Nick began to protest, but Parker held his hand up. "And before you try to take the high and mighty road and tell me that money doesn't matter, you and I know it does. Money matters—Class absolutely matters in our world. Do you think mummy Madeline will just welcome him with open arms? How soon we've forgotten what she did to darling Trixie, the last person that you wanted that was beneath you. And we're not even going to touch on him being a man. Sure, it's fashionable to date men, but it's not very practical."

"You're such a fucking snob." Nick rolled his eyes.

Parker shrugged. "Yes, I am. And so are your mother and father, both your grandparents, your siblings, and their children. I'm going easy on you, telling you the things you already know they are going to say behind your back but to his face, as they did to Trixie."

Nick sighed, letting Parker continue. "But besides that, you literally live on different sides of America. The long-distance thing is soooo cliché. Are you moving to San Francisco? Is he moving to New York? Are you both going to live in London and pretend that life is fine as long as you stay in the Mandarin? And you don't even know how he feels. What if he just wants to fuck and move on? I mean, honestly, Nicholas, do you see happily ever after with someone you met less than forty-eight hours ago?"

"I just know how I feel about him right now," said Nick. "I don't know what that means for the future. I don't even know what that means five days from now. I just know that I'm attracted to him, mind, body, heart, and spirit. And as far as how he feels about me... He feels the same. I don't know how I know, but I know."

"Well. I say leave the emotions out of it for now and just enjoy the young lad. Whatever will be will be. Go into it like that, and no one will get hurt."

Nick nodded, thankful for his friend's practical advice, but knew he was not going to take it. He finished his drink and announced, "I should get back."

"Of course, you should. Nobs don't blow themselves now, do they?"

Nick laughed and shoved his friend and kissed his face. "If this goes further, you'll stand behind me, though, won't you?"

"I have to. You make me money," Parker replied with a smile. Nick laughed and kissed his face again, then stood up and came out of the booth on the other end. "Hanson will bring you back tonight and pick you up at 8:30 a.m. sharp. The board meets at 9 a.m."

"I'll be ready. Thanks."

Parker raised his glass in acknowledgment as Nick headed out. He looked around for the pretty waitress to bring to his bed tonight, since Nick was obviously unattainable.

Nick opened the door to the penthouse, and all was quiet. It was a little after 10 p.m., and Rion was not there. He went to the second bedroom and Rion's suitcase was still there, but his book bag was gone. He breathed a sigh of relief.

Nick went to the bar and filled a glass of brandy. He sat on the terrace in the living room and quietly sipped, listening to the sounds of the night, thinking about what Parker had said to him. He hated to admit it, but his best friend was right. Rion could never fit into his world. Whatever this was, it either needed to end when he left London or needed to be casual and sporadic if they decided to keep in touch. And that thought made him incredibly sad.

He heard the door open close to midnight. Rion walked over to Nick and dropped his bag on the floor next to him. He leaned over the edge to look out and said, "I had the most amazing day."

"Tell me about it," said Nick.

Rion turned around to face him and began pacing and talking excitedly. "Brixton is inspiring. I met the most interesting people, interviewed a ton of folks that have lived there their whole lives, through the gentrification of the neighborhood. Interestingly, many people welcomed the changes while others were afraid of it losing its identity. And I get it. It's alive and rich with culture. It's... irreplaceable. I helped out in a soup kitchen and played cards in front of a grocery store. I had lunch at a Portuguese restaurant and dinner at a Caribbean soul food spot to die for. And I found it. I found the house that Darren lived in!"

"Darren?"

"My character, Darren. He grew up in Brixton and met William at boarding school. I'm changing it a bit so that William grew up in Notting Hill. They meet as roommates and fall in love."

Nick looked up, confused. "Wait, what kind of stories do you write again? I don't remember what you told me."

"Because I didn't tell you," Rion said with a smile. "I write erotic romance. Gay male erotic romance."

Nick started to laugh. "Well, okay then." Suddenly, his pen and ink tattoo made perfect sense.

Rion kept talking. "It was coming to me as I was in the cab on the way back. It's perfect. They come from two different worlds, but I'm going to make them vastly different; across race and class lines. At first, they deny their feelings, try to fight it, but it becomes—" He paused and snapped his fingers a few times.

"Magnetic," Nick finished for him.

"Yes!" Rion practically hopped. "Magnetic. That's a good word for it, thank you!"

Nick smiled. "You're welcome."

Rion started pacing again. "They go through family issues and hardships, and everyone is trying to keep them apart, saying they don't belong together. But they do. They absolutely do." He stopped again and looked at Nick. "I'm so sorry. I've been rambling. How was your meeting with your investor?"

"It was... enlightening. I'm ready for tomorrow."

"That's great, Nicky. That's so great," Rion said sincerely. "I can be there to cheer you on if you want."

"How sweet of you, Ree," Nick said sincerely back. "But it's not a big deal. And I'm sure you have plans tomorrow."

"Yeah. I'm heading to Notting Hill for a while, going to do some research up there, then back to Brixton in the evening. I got invited out to a lounge with a few people I met today."

"Look at you, making friends," Nick teased.

Rion waved him off. "You're invited to go with me tomorrow night. If... if you're not busy." Rion was still hesitant, not knowing if Nick actually wanted to do more with him than what they had been doing.

Nick smiled. "I'll let you know." Then he just remembered. "Rion, I don't have your cell number."

Rion laughed. "You don't know my last name either."

Nick was thoughtful. "Oh. Shit."

He began to laugh, and Rion laughed with him. Rion came close to him and held his hand out. Nick reached into his pocket and unlocked his phone with his fingerprint. He handed it to Rion, who added his name and phone number to his phone. Then he called it so that he had Nick's number sent to his phone, too.

"There. Now you always have access to me." He handed it back to Nick, who looked at it.

"Rion Matthews. It's a good Irish name."

"Well, I'm glad you approve. I'll make sure to let Roslyn Matthews know."

Rion kept talking excitedly about his night, and Nick watched him: His long legs going back and forth in his skinny jeans and retro Jordans, the way his arms waved around as he talked, his brown eyes wide and animated, and his smile lighting up everything around him.

Rion suddenly stopped pacing. "I'm sorry, am I, like, boring you with all this? Your eyes are kind of glossed over."

Nick said, "No, not at all. I'm just... enthralled by you."

"God, you really are a writer, too. Enthralled?" Rion asked, amused.

Nick chuckled. "I mean, yeah. I like my work, but I don't get this excited by it. You're so energizing. In a good way. In the best way."

"You are too, Nicky. Really. Everything we did yesterday, from talking on the plane to last night... I know we haven't talked about it... but this whole trip is like... I'm energized by you, too, by your presence in my life. It feels weird, but so right. Like I've known you my whole life. I'm a different person with you. You know what I mean?"

"Yes. I do. So who is Rion Matthews normally?"

Rion sighed and leaned against the terrace wall again. "Rion Matthews is just a guy who works at an indie bookstore and writes on the side. Someone who takes meds and CBD to manage his anxiety. Someone who loves his sisters and feels responsible for them, since his mother is an addict. Someone who two years ago got a lucky break when someone took an interest in one of his manuscripts and published him, and now has to live up to his own expectations. Just a regular guy from Fresno who has ended up in a fancy hotel suite with a hot, rich guy that he feels connected to. A guy he met less than three days ago that makes him fucking happy. And he's drawn to it, that feeling of simply joy. That simple connection. It's... magnetic."

They stared at each other, then Nick got up first and went over to him. Nick looked Rion in the eye as he pulled Rion's t-shirt over his head. He put his hands on Rion's hips and kissed his neck. Rion put his hand up Nick's shirt and held onto his back. Nick leaned up and kissed Rion's lips softly. Rion kissed him back more aggressively. He pulled off Nick's shirt, unbuckled his belt, and got on his knees quickly.

"Can I?" he asked as he breathed on Nick's genitals.

"Fuck yeah," Nick responded, and Rion put Nick's cock in his mouth. "Fuck, you're so good at that," Nick moaned.

Rion hummed in response. Nick held onto his head and thrust into his mouth over and over again until he was close, then Rion came off him. He grabbed his bag and said, "Come down here."

Nick did, taking off his jeans fully, and sat on the floor of the terrace. Rion pulled out a bigger bottle of Sliquid lubricant and stood up, dropping his own jeans, kicking them to the side, and putting his fingers in his own ass. Nick watched him in awe, lubricating and pleasuring himself at the same time, before Rion squatted down and wrapped the condom around Nick. He lowered himself onto Nick's cock and slid down his pole. They both moaned as their bodies fully connected.

"Did I tell you what my pen name is?" Rion asked as he put one hand on Nick's shoulder and the other on his pec and began to move.

"No..." Nick said breathlessly. "Tell me..."

"It's..." Rion moved closer to his face, "Ryan D. Ryder."

Nick started chuckling. "Oh really... Because you like to ride?"

"I *love* to ride," Rion said as he moved back and forth, up and down, rotating and grinding against Nick.

"What does the D stand for?" Nick asked, holding onto Rion's hips.

Rion said with a straight face, "Richard."

It took Nick a moment, then he bursted out in loud laughter, making Rion laugh too. But Rion took his pen name seriously and continued to bounce in Nick's lap. All Nick could do was hold on and float away into ecstasy.

Rion started moaning audibly, moving faster, calling out his lover's name, "Oh God Nicky, Oh God... you feel so good inside me... God Nicky..." Nick reached down and stroked Rion's cock for him, making him moan like a wounded animal. "Don't stop until I cum... Don't stop until I cum..." he murmured over and over again.

Nick continued to jerk Rion and Rion continued to ride until his cock pulsed in Nick's hands and cum streaked Nick's chest. The warmth of Rion's semen had Nick cumming right behind him.

Rion fell to the side of Nick with a "Holy, holy shit." He snuggled closer and put his head on Nick's shoulder, which Nick didn't mind at all.

They laid on the ground outside in silence. Nick was overwhelmed with emotions, realizing once again that he didn't want whatever he had with Rion to be casual and sporadic. He wanted to be closer to Rion, because Rion made him fucking happy, too.

He wasn't sure if the man next to him felt the same way until Rion asked in a quiet voice, "Will you hold me tonight?"

Nick looked over at Rion, but Rion wouldn't look at him. "Tonight and every night that you'll let me," he responded. He pulled Rion closer, wrapping both arms around his naked body for warmth and comfort.

*N*ick felt great coming out of the meeting with the *Parker Madison Inc.* Board of Directors. They agreed that moving to an online only platform was the wave of the future and could reach a wider variety of audiences. They made a phase-out plan for the next eighteen months and suggested putting up an international landing page for guest writers from other countries. He also added something last minute, something he did not talk with Parker about, a landing page of book reviews on erotic fiction, and the board loved that idea. Parker gave him a sly smile, but said nothing. Plans were made, contracts signed, finances were distributed, and Nick had two more years of Deep Strokez Publications.

Parker walked him out. "You were a star in there, mate. Not that I expected anything less of you. But with a new board president, a woman at that, you wooed her with that charm of yours and your speech on how most of your readers are women who enjoy their sexual liberation. Gold!"

"Thanks, Parker. As always, I appreciate your support and friendship."

Parker patted his back at the revolving doors. "So, drinks again tonight? It is Friday, after all."

Nick hesitated. "Ah... I might be busy."

Parker punched his shoulder and added, "You dirty dog you!" Nick chuckled. "Will I at least get to meet him before you hop on a plane on Monday?"

"Sure. Let's plan dinner at my hotel this weekend."

"Great plan, mate. I'll catch up with you then. And again, you were brilliant in there. Absolutely brilliant."

They hugged, and Parker went back to the elevator as Nick stepped out of the building. He pulled out his phone and sent a text.

[Nick: WYA?]

[Rion: Having tea and biscuits with the Queen.]

[Nick: No you aren't.]

[Rion: Close to it. In the middle of a tour through Buckingham Palace.]

[Nick: Cool. Want to meet somewhere for lunch?]

[Rion: Sure. Where?]

[Nick: The Roux at Parliament Square.]

[Rion: Dude, do they have burgers?]

[Nick: Absolutely not. But you won't regret me intro-
ducing you to their pork chops in romesco sauce.]

[Rion: How did you know I like pork chops? ;)]

[Nick: Call it intuition. Meet me there in one hour.]

[Rion: 👍]

It was Nick's turn to be excited when talking with
Rion at lunch. He told him about the meeting and the
enthusiasm the board president had about moving
it online and the changes they can make as a result
of it. Rion listened and added encouraging commentary, especially when discussing doing book reviews
for erotic romance.

"That's such a cool thing to do," he told Nick.

"Well, when I launch it, do you want to be a part of
it?" Nick asked in between bites.

"Like, have my novels featured?" Rion asked.

"No, like, run it. Senior editor. Get a group of indi-
viduals together to review erotic fiction to rate and
review it. Three books a month. What do you say?"

"I say, you're putting a lot of faith in someone you
met seventy-two hours ago."

Nick smiled at him. "Call it intuition."

Rion smiled. "What are you doing for the rest of
the afternoon?" Nick smiled wider. Rion laughed.
"Okay, but you'll be doing it by yourself because I'm
still going sightseeing, taking in the locals."

Nick laughed. "Want company?"

"Actually, yes. Your expensive suit fits right in with these people, so I'll just walk a half step behind you and pretend I'm your personal assistant."

"I already have one. Her name is Zoey Huffnagle, and she's phenomenal."

"Okay, well then, I'll be your executive assistant."

"His name is Marcel Delecoux, and he speaks three languages outside of English."

"Damn. Way to remind me how poor I am," Rion said with a smile.

Nick reached across the table and took his hand. "You could just walk beside me and be my friend."

Rion laced his fingers with Nick's. "With benefits?"

"You said it. I didn't, Ryder."

Rion laughed. "Let's go, Nick. I have research to do now, and then we go out tonight and unwind in Brixton. Yes?"

"Yes."

Nick ended up being Rion's tour guide, taking him to Big Ben, the Tower of London, Tower Bridge, and the British Museum. Rion pulled out his professional camera and snapped pictures, not of the landmarks but of people visiting the landmarks. He would walk up and ask politely if he could take a picture of them, and surprisingly they agreed. Rion took pictures of couples holding hands, children playing in the water, and a woman bending over and feeding the ducks. Nick loved how personable he was, striking up conversations with strangers and getting them to open up about their lives. But hadn't Rion done that for him, made him feel comfortable enough to open up during their plane ride?

They ended up walking back to Hyde Park and exploring the greenery, stopping at the Princess Diana Memorial Fountain. Rion walked around and took more pictures, even snapping one of Nick when he wasn't looking. Then he casually sat down and laid in the grass, facing the blue sky. Nick watched Rion for a moment, his eyes closed, his fingers entwined together on his abdomen, his feet crossed at the ankles.

"You're gonna burn in the sun, Irishman," Nick warned him.

"London doesn't get hot enough for that, Englishman," Rion retorted.

Nick smiled and pulled out his phone. He took a picture of Rion; then he did what he would have never done before meeting him. He took off his suit jacket and folded it up, placing it gently on the ground, took off his Tom Ford shoes, and laid down beside Rion, their shoulders touching. He looked over at his new friend, who had not budged, then he too stared at the blue sky until he closed his eyes. They laid together in silence for a while.

"If you could be anywhere in the world right now, where would it be?" Rion asked him.

"I feel like the correct answer should be right here with you," Nick said with a smile.

Rion smiled too. "This isn't a romantic comedy. I'm serious. Like... I would be on an island somewhere. Or at least somewhere where the beach is warm and so is the water. Like the Caribbean Ocean. Gabby's father was Puerto Rican, and before he died, he told us he still has a lot of family there. I promised to take her to Puerto Rico one day, and I feel like I can live up to that promise now."

Nick was thoughtful. "I think it would be the opposite for me. I want to visit Tibet and live with monks for a while in the mountains. Or a Buddhist monastery in Thailand where I can find my spiritual center. Get to know myself on a deeper level."

"You don't think you know yourself?" Rion asked.

"I think I have lived under the shadow of my siblings and my parents all my life until I decided to do this one thing for myself."

"The magazine?"

"Yup. They hate it. It's what makes me love it so much."

"Rebelling against the masses. Anarchy at its finest."

"Exactly. I find ways to piss them off with my unconventional ways."

"Like being bisexual?"

Nick hesitated. "I ... don't know. They don't necessarily know that I'm with men from time to time. They have only seen me with women."

"Well, it's good to know that this isn't something you're doing to piss off your parents."

"Doing what?"

"Doing ... *me*." Rion smiled again, and Nick smiled, too.

"No, Ryan D. Ryder, I'm not doing you to piss off my parents."

"So, then, why are you?"

Nick stayed quiet as he was thoughtful. "Because the universe threw you in my path, and I couldn't pass up the opportunity to connect with you on all levels."

"And when our path meets a crossroads, and we have to go our separate ways?"

"You said 'when,' not if."

"I know what I said."

Nick was quiet again, not liking this conversation at all, but then answered him. "If our path meets a crossroads and we go our separate ways, we will be okay. Because we've impacted each other tremendously in such a short period of time, we will never truly be separated. You'll always be a part of me, Ree."

Rion smiled again. "That was very poetic of you, Nicky."

"Well. Maybe this is a romantic comedy," Nick said.

"Yeah? How does it end?" Rion asked.

Nick did not answer. Instead, he looked over at Rion, still lying there with his eyes closed. And Nicholas did something else he would have never done. He leaned over and kissed Rion's lips softly, right on the grass in Hyde Park under the blue sky. Rion did a small intake of breath and kissed Nick back. It was soft and sweet.

Nick put his face in Rion's neck. "I'll wait to read about it in your story," he said softly.

Rion lifted his hand and touched Nick's cheek as a response.

They started out at Sequoia Shisha Bar for dinner. Rion introduced Nick to Kaleb, Lennox, Laurence and his girlfriend Rilianne, and Sonny, two women and three men of different ethnicities who Rion had hung out with the night before. Rion made sure Nick dressed down completely—in jeans and sneakers—and he loaned a black t-shirt to him. It was tighter on Nick as Rion was a tad thinner than him, but it made his muscles bulge out, so neither Nick nor Rion minded. Rion also chose jeans and a dark blue t-shirt with white lettering that said, "The Future is Female."

They sat next to each other, but not so close as to make it seem like they were a couple. Their new friends asked questions about how Nick and Rion had met, and he simply said, "We met on a plane, and he asked me if I needed a place to crash." Rion did it on purpose, not wanting it to be known they were intimate, and was prepared to put space between them. But Rion surprised Nick with how little attention he paid to him throughout the night. Nick was grateful for his discretion at first, but then felt a little slighted. Lennox proved to be a good distraction from his feelings, as she kept talking and flirting with him, and Rion pretended like he didn't notice.

After a dinner of the Caribbean delicacy of stewed beef in a savory sauce, Kaleb stated first, "Let's take the night someplace else. Ever been to Brixton Courtyard?"

"I have been once," Nick admitted. "It's a cool place."

"With who?" Rion asked curiously.

Nick smiled. "This isn't my first time in the city."

"God, I *love* your accent," Lennox mused and flipped her wavy brown hair. "It's so ... serious." She leaned over and touched his arm, and he turned his attention to her. "Are you always so serious?"

Rion watched Nick allow her to rub his arm out of the corner of his eyes. "Not always," he replied.

"Well, good. Save a dance for me at the Courtyard, yeah?" She batted her eyelashes at him.

"Sure, first dance goes to you," Nick flirted with her back.

"Let's go then," said Rilianne happily.

She stood up and grabbed Laurence's hand to lead the way. Nick ended up in the car with Lennox and Sonny, while Rion hopped in the backseat of Laurence's car with Rilianne and Kaleb. He tried really hard not to think about what they were doing in the backseat of Sonny's car, but the more he thought about it, the more he was annoyed at Nick, although he knew he had no right to be.

Brixton Courtyard turned out to be exactly what it sounded like, an outdoor seating area with a live band playing music and people dancing around in between tables. Rion struck up a conversation with Laurence while Lennox threw all her attention at Nick and talked about America. He almost rolled his eyes every time she gushed over the word, "I just love *American* news reporters, and I would love to go to an *American* amusement park, and are the buildings taller in *America*?"

It frustrated him how much attention Nick paid to her, but Nick wasn't his to claim, so instead, he nursed his beer and watched them dance closely and talk in each other's ear.

"You look like someone who lost his best mate," Kaleb said, sitting down next to him with his third vodka and cranberry, and taking Rion out of his thoughts. Kaleb was a dark-skinned and muscular black Brit, whose life outside of being a train conductor consisted of drinking, partying, and finding the joy in life. He flipped back his long dreadlocks that had shells attached to some of the ends and waited for Rion's response.

"I'm good, man," Rion said casually, also on his third drink.

They quietly watched the crowd together, and then Kaleb spoke again. "My older brother is gay, you know. Did I tell you that?"

"No," Rion replied. "I don't think it's come up."

"Yeah, he's a meaty bloke like me. Most people don't know that about him. Except me, I've always known. Especially the way he used to stare at our next door neighbor, the boy with the perfect brown eyes. He confessed to me."

"Hmmm," Rion murmured and continued to sip his Guinness.

"I used to tell him, if you want him, Alex, just go get him. The worst that can happen is he rejects you, but at least you'll stop torturing yourself, mate." Rion turned to look Kaleb in the eye, and Kaleb did not back down. "Anyway, that's my brother. He's come into his own now, married and all. So it all worked out for him, innit?"

He patted Rion's shoulder and rose up to go to the bar and grab another drink. Rion took a sip of his beer and let his eyes wander back over to Nick and Lennox. She absolutely wanted him. And he was absolutely sure if he wasn't with Nick, it would be her in his bed tonight. But Rion was there, so she wouldn't be. That thought made him feel a little better.

"What are you so happy about, mate?" Sonny came over and asked as he sat in the seat that Kaleb had just occupied. Sonny was Korean born but adopted into a British family as a baby. He and Kaleb were best friends.

"Nothing, man, just taking in the view," he said casually.

"Yeah, well, the view here is gobby. I'm heading over to a Reggaeton club in a few. You're down?"

"Yeah, that sounds like fun. Let me see what Nick wants to do."

"Nick wants to do Lennox," Sonny joked. "Let's go find you a fit bird to fancy tonight."

Rion smiled through his annoyance. "Not looking for any women, but dancing sounds fun."

"Cheers. Let me grab the others."

Sonny stood up and went looking for Rilianne and Laurence. Nick and Lennox came to the table holding hands a few minutes later. "Sonny said we're going to I Love Reggaeton, yeah?" she asked excitedly.

But Rion's eyes were glued to their hands. He slowly looked up at Nick, who caught his eye. Nick shook his head slightly, pleading for understanding in his eyes. *It's not what you think*, they told Rion. Nick gently tried to pull his hand away, but Lennox absent-mindedly pulled back, tightening her grip.

Rion rolled his eyes and answered her. "Yeah, we're going. Let me go get Kaleb." He stood up abruptly and walked away from Nick and his new girlfriend.

When they entered the Reggaeton club, there was instant energy. Everyone was dancing against each other; the spinning strobe lights were the only color on the crowded and dark dance floor. The music was so loud that the bass was pumping through their bodies, from their feet all the way up. Rilianne and Laurence disappeared quickly, and Kaleb went for the bar, obviously not drunk enough from the Courtyard.

Before Nick could turn to Rion and whisper something in his ear, Lennox grabbed his hand again.

"Dance with me, yeah!" she screamed at him over the music and dragged him toward the middle of the room.

Nick glanced back at Rion helplessly, who gave him a small nod and turned away, following Kaleb to the bar. Rion didn't want to be jealous, but he was. It was a reminder that Nick was more straight than bi, that he dates women, but has sex with men, occasionally. Rion was something of an occasion for Nick. He had been fine with that when they first started the affair. He was even fine with it all day as they hung out. But the more Nick ignored Rion and paid attention to the beautiful Lennox, the more he realized he was no longer fine with it. And he hated feeling that way. Rion regretted keeping his distance from Nick tremendously and wished he had grabbed Nick's hand and kissed him as they sat down for dinner, making it known that Nick belonged to him.

Kaleb was already ordering something when Rion approached. He wordlessly handed Rion his drink and ordered another. Rion took one sip, and the sourness of it almost made him spit it out. "What is that?" he mouthed to his new friend.

Kaleb moved closer to his ear and yelled, "Spicy Poblano Lemonade Bomb. Scrummy, innit?"

Rion's eyes went wide to display how not scrummy it was. Kaleb laughed and said, "Drink it fast. Trust me, mate." He pushed the plastic cup to Rion's lips again.

Rion shook his head, but took a big gulp. It burned going down his throat but left a sweet aftertaste. "That's fucking awesome!" he found himself yelling.

"Cheers!" Kaleb yelled back and pushed their cups together.

They downed the first one, and Kaleb ordered three more each. Rion felt much better after the fourth one. He followed Kaleb to the dance floor, and women immediately flocked to them both, running their hands through Kaleb's brown locks and touching all over Rion's body, moving their bottoms against his groin. Rion held onto the woman in front of him by her hips and moved along with her. She was an expert, wining her waist in a circular motion with the beat, and when she turned around, she hiked her already short skirt up, straddled his right leg, and rubbed her vagina up and down against his thigh. The woman wrapped her arms around his neck, and he moved his hands up around her back, pulling her closer. Not because he was interested in her, but because he wanted to feel a body up against him. But she started getting handsy, pressing her hard nipples against his chest, pulling his face down, and when he turned it, she started kissing on his neck. Kaleb turned around from the woman he was dancing with and started pushing his groin against Rion's dance partner. He pulled her backward toward him and winked at Rion.

Rion mouthed, "Thank you," and slowly danced away.

More women danced with him, which he didn't mind. He caught the eye of a man watching him, but turned around and danced in the opposite direction. Suddenly, Nick and Lennox were in front of him. She was holding onto his neck, and he had his hands wrapped around her back as they whispered to each other. They looked ... intimate. Rion realized he had stopped dancing and was staring. As if he sensed it, Nick looked up and caught the look on his face. He pulled Lennox's hands from around his neck.

"Rion!" he called over the music.

Rion turned around and walked back the way he came. After a few steps, the man that was eyeing him was standing there, tall, blond, with spiky hair and thin lips. He stepped closer to Rion and said in his ear, "Want to dance, handsome?"

Rion started moving against him as his answer. The man smiled and moved with him, pulling him close against his body, similar to what he had done with the first woman he danced with, and the blond man allowed it. He put his cheek on Rion's, and they danced together. Rion decided to turn around, and the man wrapped his arms around Rion's sculptured abs and pressed his hard cock on Rion's bottom. Rion let him do it, feeling inebriated and silly about his feelings for Nick. His eyes were lidded, so he barely recognized it when Nick came up to them.

They stared at each other, then Nick held his hand out. "Ree," he mouthed.

Rion didn't want to go with him. Nick was going to hurt him; he was sure of it. But every time the light hit Nick's blue wanting eyes, his resolve waned. Rion took his hand, and Nick caressed it, then Nick yanked him hard, pulling him forcefully away from his male dance partner. The man was startled by the sudden movement. Rion fell completely against Nick's chest, and Nick held him tightly, locking his arms around his back. They looked at each other, then Nick looked beyond Rion at the spiky blond and gave him a menacing glare. The man immediately backed away.

He looked back down at Rion's wide brown eyes. Rion slowly slid his hand up Nick's back and put his head into Nick's neck. Rion licked his lips and kissed him there a few times. They swayed to the beat of the music together. Nick's hands made it to Rion's butt, squeezing his cheeks, pushing their groins together, both feeling the heat between them. Rion lifted his head, and Nick immediately brought his lips down on him, pulling his bottom lip. Rion slid his tongue between Nick's lips. They licked each other's tongues and continued to move together, holding each other. One song passed, then two, then three. Then they lost count of the songs playing. There was no one else around them that they were aware of, only the intensity of their attraction and their bodies against each other.

Finally, Rion said in his ear, "If it's me you want, then take me home, Nicky."

Nick didn't hesitate. He turned them both around and laced his fingers with Rion, pulling him through the crowd. He saw Lennox dancing with Sonny, but when she glanced at them, he turned his head. Rion caught Kaleb's eye by the bar again and nodded, letting him know they were leaving, and Kaleb held his cup up as an acknowledgment with a huge smile. They stepped out of the club, and the night air hit them both, cooling them down.

Nick held firmly to Rion's hand and hailed a cab. He slid Rion in first, then got in behind him, saying, "The Mandarin Oriental, Hyde Park."

Rion barely waited for the cab to pull off when he attacked Nick, biting his lip in a kiss, digging his nails into the nape of his neck, and yanking his hair. Nick let him be as aggressive as he wanted to be. He felt Rion's anger, his desire, his frustration, his need to claim Nick back from someone that could give him what he couldn't. Nick let him draw blood with his nails on his neck and bite him again, communicating how he felt about him. But then he pulled Rion's face back and held his chin firmly, giving him eye contact. Nick squeezed Rion's cheeks and forced his tongue into his mouth aggressively, and grabbed Rion's cock through his jeans, giving it a squeeze. Nick held his face and continued to rub his cock. He kissed him repeatedly, communicating right back how he felt about him, soothing Rion's anger, reassuring him with his hands and mouth, kissing his face, cheeks, and forehead until he felt Rion relent and go limp in his arms. Nick pulled him close and cradled his head to his chest, and Rion held on tight, his breath labored, his eyes closed, taking in Nick's cologne and natural body scent through his sweat. He relaxed as Nick rubbed his hair and kissed his forehead every few moments until the cab pulled up in front of the luxury hotel.

Nick paid the driver wordlessly, held onto Rion's hand tightly, and pulled him from the car. They walked through the hotel hand in hand and waited for the elevator together in silence. They didn't look at each other as they held hands in the elevator all the way to the suite. Nick used one hand to swipe his keycard and open the door, and led Rion to the master bedroom. Rion stood before him, a little drunk and a lot emotionally exhausted from the night. Nick slowly pulled off Rion's t-shirt, unbuckled his belt, and zipped down his pants. He bent down and took off Rion's Jordans, then his socks. Nick stood back up and slid Rion's jeans down one leg at a time, stood up again, and slid off Rion's briefs. Rion was completely naked in front of him, strong and beautiful. Nick waited.

Rion stepped closer and took off Nick's black t-shirt. He touched Nick's chest, rubbing his pecs and melting his fingers through his hair, then touched his abs, his shoulders and his arms. He moved in for a lingering kiss, then began to take off Nick's jeans, too, but forgot to take off his sneakers as Nick's pants dropped down.

Rion giggled drunkenly. "Oh. Right." Nick smiled.

Rion tried to bend down but realized he would topple over, so he sat down on the floor instead. Nick sat at the edge of the bed and looked down at how childlike Rion seemed, sitting cross-legged on the floor, unlacing his sneakers. Rion took his time, sliding them off his feet one by one, then removed Nick's socks. He pulled each pant leg from him and crumpled Nick's jeans behind him before he swung his legs around and came into a kneeling position in front of him. Nick ran his fingers through Rion's curls a few times as Rion slid off his boxer briefs before he leaned down to kiss his lips softly. Then Nick reached below Rion's underarms and pulled him into the bed with him.

Nick rolled Rion onto his back, kissing and touching him. Then Rion spoke. "Lennox. She's beautiful."

Nick ran his hands through Rion's hair again. "Yes. She's beautiful."

"Very beautiful."

"Yes."

"You want to sleep with her," Rion stated.

"No," Nick said automatically. "She wanted to sleep with me. She told me to take her home. I told her no. I told her I already had someone in my bed. Then I looked up and saw you."

"But if I wasn't here, you would have brought her here."

"Yes," Nick admitted. "But you are here. And I don't want anyone else but you. You're the one I want." Nick kissed Rion's lips. "If you and I are in the same room, in the same space, you'll always be the one that I want."

"Don't say things like that," Rion whispered.

Nick got off Rion and went to the nightstand. He grabbed a condom and the lube and crawled back onto the bed on his knees between Rion. Instead of telling him, he was going to show him.

He started at Rion's calves, kissing them all the way up to his thighs, taking his time and alternating between legs. Nick licked the sweaty creases between Rion's groin and thigh, licked up his rod, and put it in his mouth. Rion groaned. Nick's mouth continued to bob on Rion's cock, making it nice and wet before he went lower and licked Rion's round and dark pink balls and put each in his mouth. Rion began to stroke himself, but Nick gently took his hand away. He went farther down and licked his taint before pushing his legs completely up and licking the sweat between his cheeks, digging his tongue in until he found the entrance he was looking for.

Rion cried out his name, "Nicky!" and held his legs up completely for him. Nick held onto his cheeks and ate Rion's bottom with fervor and urgency, as if he would never get to do it again.

"Oh God, Nicky, oh God!" Rion called out his name over and over again, only fueling Nick's desire to please him to the max. He came up only once to lick the cum dripping from his cock, more bitter than bleachy like the day before, and went back to Rion's ass until Rion started begging, "Please, Nicky, please, please..."

Nick came all the way up, licking his torso along the way, and stuck his tongue in Rion's mouth. Rion accepted hungrily, tasting his own musk, and pulled at Nick's hair. Nick pulled back only an inch and said, "Who does Nicky want?"

Rion let a couple of quick breaths pass, getting lost in Nick's blue eyes. "Me?" he asked hesitantly.

Nick shook his head. "You don't believe it yet. I'm going to make you believe it."

Before Rion could talk again, Nick went back into a kneeling position between Rion's legs. He squirted gel onto his fingers and massaged the outside of Rion's already open hole before he inserted them inside. It was already wet with Nick's saliva, but the gel made it silky wet. Rion moaned loudly as Nick's fingers made their way to his prostate. He felt the small hump, and Rion's entire body shivered. Rion immediately went to grab his cock, but again, Nick pulled his fingers off. He rubbed gently inside of him, and Rion's cock continued to leak translucent pre-cum against his abs, running in between the creases. Nick leaned over and licked his belly, then moved back up to lick Rion's tongue again.

Rion wanted Nick so badly, more than the first time. He murmured again, "Please, Nicky, please..."

"Please, what?" Nick asked as he ground his cock against Rion's, licking his neck and putting his tongue in his ear.

"Please… fuck me."

Nick smiled and kissed his cheek. He would do no such thing.

Nick leaned up once more and grabbed the condom off the bed. Rion patiently waited for Nick to cover his cock. When the task was completed, he held Rion's legs up and slowly inserted himself inside, making Rion groan. He put Rion's legs against his chest, his feet on his shoulders, and began to move his waist back and forth, his cock all the way in, pulled back to the head, then to the hilt again.

Rion's entire body was tingling, every nerve awake. Nick's steady lovemaking meant everything to him at that moment. He realized Nick wanted him to know how much he cared about him, that Rion was not just a quick fuck, but someone he wanted, possibly needed.

He moaned out his name again, "Nick…"

"Who does Nicky want?" Nick asked again.

"Me… Nicky wants… me."

Nick sighed. He put both of Rion's legs to the left of him and continued his steady pace. "Nicky will always want Ree. Say it."

"Nicky … wants … Ree." Rion managed to get out between breaths. He was already close. He reached down again for his cock, but again, Nick took his hand away, holding it tight.

"No," he said simply.

"I need to cum," Rion moaned out.

"You will cum," Nick told him. He angled his body so that he put more pressure on Rion's internal nub and moved faster.

"Oh, God…" Rion tried to pull his hand out of Nick's grasp, but Nick held tighter.

"Cum for me," Nick demanded. He held onto the side of Rion's thigh, and his other hand held onto Rion's tightly. "Let go and cum for me."

Rion could barely talk, his mind going completely blank as his orgasm rolled through his body. He let out a "Fuuuuck," right before his cock began to pump out ropes of cum unassisted right onto the bed in front of him. "Mmm... Mmm... Mmmmm," he kept moaning until his ropes lessened to smaller strings, leaving his cock weeping. He had never cum so hard in all his life.

Nick gave him a moment to recover from the high of his climax, then pulled out and pushed Rion onto his stomach. He slid in quickly and began to pump up and down, jack-hammering Rion. Rion cried out but arched his back so that the groove at his tailbone was deeper, and he took it. He felt all of Nick's passion for him, and he wanted it. Nick grunted and thrust quickly until his balls pulled up. He pulled out and took off his condom right before his cock started spewing cum across Rion's back. He fell back against the lower part of the bed, exhausted and satiated.

Rion crawled down to Nick and licked the remnants of cum from his leaking cock before he rested his head against Nick's shoulder and put his arm around his torso. Nick rubbed his cum like lotion into Rion's skin on his back, then found his bottom, squeezing, kneading, and gently tapping it.

Rion spoke first. "Nicky will always want Ree."

Nick smiled and repeated, "Nicky will always want Ree."

*R*ion woke up alone in Nick's bed and immediately put his hand on his aching head. He remembered the night before, but wished he didn't. He had held it together until Kaleb introduced him to that spicy lemonade, and then he lost all sense of himself. Jealousy and anger reared their heads, turning into emotion and submission for a man that he barely knew. Today was day four. In two days, Nick was getting on a plane, going back to his life, and Rion was hopping over to Kaleb's house in Brixton and going on with his. In two days, this would all be over.

*This is not a thing*, he told himself. He couldn't get sucked in. Despite the intense attraction, the yearning for each other, the ease and comfort they felt around each other, the trust they foolishly and ignorantly had for each other, despite all that, it wouldn't, *couldn't* be a thing. Rion was better than that, smarter than to fall for someone so out of his league. And yet...

He got off the bed and took a shower in the huge walk-in, frosted glass shower door. Bits and pieces of their lovemaking came back to him. It was the only way he could describe it, as lovemaking. Every time they did it, it became more and more emotional. Intimate. Bonding. Rion decided he needed to move back into the spare bedroom and stop having sex with Nick. Amazing, mind-blowing, orgasm-producing, climactic, intense sex with Nick. He needed to stop Nick from running his fingers through his hair, kissing his neck, licking him between his cheeks, cupping his balls, and putting his steel rod deep inside of him over and over again...

And Rion realized there was no way he could stop having sex with Nick.

"I'm fucked," Rion said out loud.

He sighed, thinking of Nick's words: "If you and I are in the same space, you'll always be the one I want. Nicky will always want Ree."

Mentally, he wondered how true that was, but his heart and his body were already all in. He turned the handle to cool off and finished his shower. He wrapped a towel around his waist, came out of the bathroom, grabbed his clothes off the floor, then slipped out across the hall to the room he was supposed to be occupying. He paused upon hearing Nick on the phone. He was speaking in a low tone, so Rion couldn't make out the words. It was the first time he had considered that Nick could have an actual girlfriend.

He sighed again and went into the room, closing the door behind him, and leaned against it. "I'm so fucked," he told himself again.

Rion got dressed and came out of the bedroom to see that Nick was still on the phone. He smiled at Rion when he saw him and pointed to the table, which already had breakfast waiting.

"Yeah... Okay, great. Hey Sarah, I have to go, but I'll call you when we're on our way, okay? Okay, great, cheers." Nick hung up as Rion stood by the table. He came over and put his arms around Rion's back. They kissed softly.

"Good morning."

"Morning," Rion responded.

"How do you feel?"

"Like I had way too much to drink last night."

Nick laughed. "You did. But it's okay. I'll take care of you."

Rion shook his head, but smiled. "I don't need you to take care of me, Nicholas." He moved away and sat at the table.

Nick felt the cold shoulder, and it worried him, but he said nothing. They sat at the table together in silence and began to eat. He watched Rion silently spread cream cheese to his everything bagel, add smoked salmon, tomatoes, eggs, and bacon to it, then stuff his face.

"Wow. Never took you for a lox sandwich kind of guy," Nick teased, breaking the silence.

"I have a thing for cream cheese," Rion spoke with his mouth full. "I have an ex that introduced me to it a long time ago."

He held it out, and Nick took a bite. Rion watched the way his mouth formed around the sandwich and as Nick pulled back from it, leaving cream cheese on his bottom lip. Rion forgot himself for a moment, leaned over and licked it, then pressed their lips together. His lips lingered, surprising Nick with how hot and cold he was being, but then Rion stopped abruptly.

Rion tried to lean back. "We shouldn't... I shouldn't have—"

"Yes, you should." Nick quickly grabbed his face and pulled him back to lick his tongue.

"Nicky," he moaned out as Nick moved to his neck and kissed him there.

"Don't pull away, Rion, please," he murmured in his ear. "Not yet. I only have two more days here. Two more days, and if you never want to see me again, you don't have to. Just let it be what it is right now. Please, Ree?"

"Oh God, I am so incredibly fucked, aren't I?" Rion said quietly.

"I think we both are," Nick said, coming out of his neck and kissing his mouth again. "Don't pull away, okay? I just want to feel everything that I feel with as much intensity as I feel it, for once in my life. Can you do that with me?"

"Okay, Nick," Rion agreed. "I can do that with you."

"Good." Nick kissed his lips once more and moved his hands to Rion's thighs, rubbing them. "I have a full day planned for us. A family friend of mine, Sarah, lives in Kensington, and we're going to visit her first. She has a friend that sells real estate in the Royal Borough, so he's going to take us in and out of the homes for sale there, so you can get a sense of how the other half lives for William."

Rion was shocked. "Wow. I can't believe you're doing that for me."

"That's not all I'm doing," Nick said. "I changed my room reservation to the end of June. I want more than anything to stay here with you, but I have to get back. I have some work obligations back home and meetings to attend. But you can stay here. The room is paid up for the month, and anything you need, food, car service, a damn pedicure and massage, you have access to it. Just charge it to the room."

Rion's mouth dropped completely. "Nick... oh... no... you... no."

"It's already done," Nicholas said definitively. "You can absolutely choose to leave when I leave, but the room is just going to be sitting here, unoccupied, for the rest of the month."

"Why did you do that?" Rion whined.

"Because I care about you, Ree. Because I like that I make you happy. Because I want to make you feel as special as you make me feel. Because I think I'm—"

He stopped himself from saying too much, but Rion already knew what he had almost let slip. It would be crazy of either of them to say it out loud. They had only known each other for four days. There was no way they could feel that strongly about each other. But Rion felt it, too.

Nick's face began to turn pink from embarrassment, so Rion rescued him by kissing him passionately. They pulled at each other's lips and caressed their chests, arms, and thighs. Rion pulled back first and asked, "What time are we heading out?"

"Whenever you're ready," Nick said.

"I need a shower first."

"I thought you already showered," Nick asked curiously. "I heard the water going."

"We're gonna need another one," Rion said seriously.

Nick smiled and grabbed his hand to pull him to the couch.

After a quick but intense sexual connection and another shower, this time together, Nick called the car service to take them to the Kensington section of London, one of the most affluent places Rion had ever seen. Rion noticed they could have walked and vowed to make sure they walked back to the hotel. They stopped at a large home that looked like Rion's entire family could fit into it.

They got out of the car, but then Nick turned to him. "So, she doesn't know that I'm ... not completely straight."

Rion chuckled. "Oh. Okay, got it. No kissing in front of company."

Nick leaned over and kissed his cheek, then walked them up the stairs to the huge, white wooden door. Nick rang the doorbell, and a mature blonde woman answered.

"Nicholas. It's so wonderful to see you."

"Lovely to see you too, Sarah. I'm so glad you could do this for me."

"Of course, darling, you're practically family." They kissed each other's cheek as a little boy ran up to her legs. "And here's Henry, the nosy one. Andrew has found better interest in his cars, obviously."

"The twins are so big," Nicholas exclaimed. "Last time I saw Caroline, they were babies."

"All of five years old now. And well, that's because you keep yourself away, my dear. Emma and Caroline summer in the Hamptons together." She looked beyond Nick and said, "You must be Rion, the writer."

"Yes, nice to meet you, Sarah," Rion answered. She leaned in to kiss his cheek as well.

"Charmed. Come in, come in, now." She led the way, and Nick and Rion followed her.

Immediately upon entering, Rion tried hard not to be completely impressed. He kept his mouth from dropping open at the huge crystal and glass chandelier above their heads. There was an elevator in the home, with numbers one through five. They walked past rooms upon rooms in the long but spacious hallway until they came to the opening of a contemporary living room area with glass accordion doors that opened to another seating area in a large garden. Nick and Sarah chatted, keeping up on the latest family news, leaving Rion to wander around the main area.

He walked outside and stood in the closed yard, hidden from the neighbors by high bushes on all sides. He was correct when he thought his entire family could fit on this one floor, and they had five floors.

Nick and Sarah met him out there. "Oh, good, you found the tea," Sarah said, pointing at the table.

Rion noticed the fancy tea set sitting over literal tea light candles. He didn't even know that was what tea lights were actually for, keeping tea warm. He stood staring at it when Sarah asked him a question.

"Huh?" He snapped his head up. "I'm sorry, I didn't hear."

"I was asking if you wanted a tour first, dear. That is why you're here, right? To look at properties for inspiration for your newest novel? I do hope you choose this one. Victor and I take great pride in being able to raise our children in the same home his family has owned for generations. But Ian is sure to show you some contenders."

"Ah... yeah. I mean, yes," he said, remembering his manners. "A tour would be nice."

"Wonderful." She clapped her hands. "Andrew, want to take a walk with Grammy?"

A little boy that looked exactly like the other one still hanging onto his grandmother's leg appeared from behind one of the chairs in the living room with his toy car. "Yes, Grammy."

Sarah smiled. "I just knew they would want to come along. They aren't allowed in certain areas of the home, so this is their only opportunity to see them. We'll start our way at the top and make our way down, shall we?"

They stood at the elevator, and Rion asked, "Why aren't the children allowed in certain spaces?"

"Well, they're for the adults, obviously. You'll see."

The elevator came, and they piled in. After a short moment, it dinged, and the five of them entered the hallway on the fifth floor. There was a gate at the top of the stairs.

"There are two bedrooms and two bathrooms on this floor, large and airy with natural light. This is where Andrew and Henry sleep."

Rion looked into both rooms with queen-size beds in them. They didn't look like children's bedrooms at all, but it reminded him of his guest bedroom at the Mandarin. "Upstairs is another room we have made into their play area."

"So you have six floors?" Rion asked.

"Indeed. Go on, see for yourself. The elevator does not go up there," Sarah said, pointing at the stairs.

Rion traveled up the narrow stairs to see the room that could be a bedroom but had toy bins and shelves for toys. Most of the toys were scattered around. "Wow," he breathed out. It became evident that the children were sent upstairs so that the rest of the home could remain immaculate. To be seen and not heard.

But Rion came down with a smile. "It's very nice."

She beamed. "I thought you would like it. Come now. We have many things to discover."

They traveled using the stairs, going down with Sarah discussing each room, its purpose, and the names of the designers that decorated it. On the fourth floor was the entire master suite, with a walk-in closet the size of a large bedroom, the master bedroom, two bathrooms, and a sitting area. The fourth floor was bigger than Rion's one-bedroom apartment.

Sarah said, "It used to be three rooms here, but we simply opened it up and made it our own personal paradise."

They skipped the third floor, which was the main floor they had come in on, and went down to the second floor. They went to the right first, where there was another bedroom and bath, a small kitchenette, and a wine cupboard. To the left was another open area with a full kitchen, a living room, and a game room.

"This is the family room," she explained. "Where we spend most of our time."

"Do the kids come down here to play?" Rion asked.

Sarah grimaced. "Oh, heaven's no. You've seen their play area, haven't you? It's all they'll ever need." She changed the subject. "Come now, one more exciting feature."

They took the elevator down one more flight to the basement. Rion did not know what to expect, but he did not expect what he saw. "Holy, holy shit," he said quietly.

They stepped off the elevator into what resembled a large spa. There was a gym on one side, showers, and a sauna on the other side, and in the middle of the room was an expansive indoor pool that ran the length of the room. "What's the square footage of the home?"

"Ten thousand, nine hundred and thirty-five," she said proudly.

"Wow," Rion replied. Sarah waited. "Oh, it's definitely a contender for my novel. It's exactly the way I pictured William growing up, in a large … house." Rion could not describe it as a home for a family.

"Wonderful!" she beamed again. "Let's have tea, shall we? I'm also making fresh scones."

They took the elevator back up to the third floor and sat outside in the garden. The boys began to run around in the yard as Sarah poured tea and continued to make small talk, asking Rion where he was from, "California," what kind of writing he did, "Contemporary Romance," and if he and Nick had met through the course of work, "No, but he did offer me a job."

"That's Nicholas for you, always helping others out. If only Madeline could see it that way."

Rion asked, "Madeline?"

"My mother," Nick answered him. "Nothing that I could ever do would be right in her eyes."

"Oh, that's not true," Sarah chided. "She recognizes your success, albeit from a different path than she had envisioned you on." Nick snorted a laugh. "And she approves of Penelope. How is that dear girl?"

Rion sensed it automatically, Nick's tension. Nick drank a gulp of tea, then responded with a simple, "She's fine."

"Oh, good. I was surprised Penny didn't come along the trip with you this time."

"No, she had some other business to attend to in Canada," he said conversationally and sipped again, avoiding Rion's curious eyes.

"Well, she is a woman on the move. You're lucky to have her. Send her my regards."

"I will, thank you."

The oven bell went off as if on cue, and Sarah rose from her seat. "The scones are ready. We'll let them cool off a bit and then serve them warm. More tea?"

"No, thank you, Sarah."

"I'm fine, too, thanks," Rion chimed in.

Sarah left the area, and Rion and Nick sat quietly until Rion asked, much calmer than he felt, "Who's Penny?"

Nick didn't respond. Rion turned to look at him. Nick slowly turned to look at Rion. "Fuck," Rion said quietly and turned his head.

Nicholas sighed. "Rion—"

"Are you married?" Rion cut him off and asked.

"No."

"Girlfriend?"

"Kind of."

"Kind of?"

"It's ... complicated."

"Complicated. Right." Rion sighed. "Why didn't you tell me?"

"Because you didn't ask. And I didn't ask about you, either."

"Well, I'm single."

"Okay. And I'm in a situation that I've been trying to get myself out of for almost two years."

"Two years!?" Rion turned to him in disbelief.

"Like I said, it's complicated," Nick stated. "She isn't someone that I'm in love with or even see a future with. But I can't walk away just yet." Rion shook his head and sighed through his nose in frustration.

"Look at me," Nick demanded. Rion did. "You're telling me you've never been in a situation that was hard to walk away from?" Rion's mind immediately went to Jason, who he had been on and off with for the last three years. Nick saw his eyes change and said, "That, right there! Whoever that person was that came to mind means you understand complicated."

Rion's face softened. "I understand complicated."

Nick slid his hand over to Rion's on the couch and touched it. "This is the first time in a long time that I've felt something for someone. And I know you feel it, too. So stop finding reasons to pull away from me. Please, Ree," he begged quietly.

Rion melted under Nick's touch. Instead of responding, he flipped his hand over and squeezed Nick's hand. Nick squeezed back; then they let go.

Sarah came back a few moments later, and the boys ran to the area, but before they sat down, she chided, "Go wash your hands and return, please."

They obediently obeyed their grandmother, and the three adults sat silently, waiting for the boys to return. Once they did, Sarah cut the bread into fourths and served it on little plates to everyone.

"I'm surprised that you don't have a maid for this," Rion said and then instantly regretted it.

Sarah looked up sharply, but then remembered herself and smiled. "Greta is our house manager, and she is off on Saturdays."

Rion nodded, knowing he had overstayed his welcome. He stayed quiet as Nick and Sarah continued talking. About forty minutes later, the doorbell chimed, and Sarah went to open it with Henry running behind her. "Oh Ian, good, right on time," he heard Sarah say.

Rion turned to Nick. "We should get going. The day is getting away from us."

"Yeah, let's do that. We have plans tonight. I invited Parker for dinner."

"Your investor? Guess I should try to make a good impression, huh?"

Nick reached over quickly, squeezed his hand, and let go as Sarah and Ian walked over. "Just be you," he whispered, then rose to shake Ian's hand.

Ian Wells turned out to be a really nice guy; personable, funny, and knowledgeable. He told them, "The thing is, you'll see more flats for sale than actual properties. Flat living is the way to go here, with 24-hour concierge and spa services."

But Rion quickly learned that the "flats" of the wealthy were nothing like any of the apartments he had ever been in. The smallest one was 1600 square feet, and the largest one was a 4000 square-foot penthouse apartment with four bedrooms and four baths. The price tags never went below five million pounds for any of the ones they looked at. He took out his notebook and took notes on the features he wanted to include. When they stopped at a five-bedroom, four-bath flat that was going for twenty-three million pounds, he had had enough of looking at how the rich lived. He stopped in one of the bedrooms, furnished but cold and impersonal, and looked out into the street.

Nick came behind him and rubbed his shoulders. "You're very pensive today."

"Did you grow up like this?" Rion questioned him. "In a large and airy home with areas that you were restricted from going? No ... love?"

Nick paused his rubbing and said, "Yes."

"How did you survive it?" Rion asked.

"I just ... did. My father wasn't exactly cold, but he isn't a hugger. My mother is cold. I got more hugs from the au pairs than from my actual parents. They put expectations on us from the moment we were born to act a certain way, to achieve greatness, and to never embarrass them. I achieved greatness in my own right, but I embarrassed them with how, so we're not close. Not that we ever were, but at least now it's a little better, mostly because I've given in to some things. Like being with Penny."

The name Penny made Rion's heart lurch, but he ignored it. Instead, Rion turned around and kissed Nick on the lips. "I'm done looking at homes. Let's walk back."

Nick returned the kiss. "Okay, Ree."

*N*ick reached over for Rion's hand a couple of blocks into their slow walk, and Rion allowed it. They walked in silence, enjoying each other's company, with Rion only letting go when he received inspiration and needed to take a picture. They walked around Hyde Park again, still holding hands like old lovers. Rion's mind was going in a million different directions, so he welcomed the silence. He definitely felt more at home in Brixton, the culture, the diversity, and the love he felt from the people. But stepping into a world that was so far from his own was fascinating, too.

He wanted to interview Nick but wasn't sure if he should today. Nick had revealed so much about himself and his life by saying so little, and he didn't want to push him too much. More than anything, Rion wanted to wrap Nick up in his arms and hold on to him. Rion had discovered that Nick was desperate for a connection. A connection he was not getting from his parents and probably never had; a connection he didn't seem to be getting from Penelope—there was a story there; a connection he had found with Rion, and he wanted to hold on to it for as long as he could. And if Rion was honest with himself, he too wanted this connection, needed it. He understood exactly how Nick was feeling, allowing himself to let go and feel all the intensity he wanted to feel for once in his life.

Rion had always been careful to keep his emotions in check. He had to when dealing with Roslyn, who had brought nothing but anguish into his life from the day she gave birth to him, and he had to be strong for his sisters. But Nicholas made him feel like he could let go completely and he would be there to catch him. It was silly and unreal to feel this way, and yet it felt so serious and so real to him, to them both. He hadn't been in a serious relationship since Jason, which had technically ended eight months ago, but since they still sleep together from time to time, it made it impossible to move on. But in the three years of being together, Jason had never made Rion feel close to how he had felt in the last four days with Nicky. Nicholas was a gift, and he was going to take all of it and enjoy it for the next couple of days.

In the elevator going up to the penthouse, Nick said, "We have a couple of hours until dinner. Parker will meet us downstairs at eight."

"Okay. I have some writing to do, if that's okay. I need to get down the ideas that are in my head right now."

"Okay. I'll give you your space."

"No, you don't have to," Rion said. "In fact, I would like to interview you. Get a glimpse of what life was like for you growing up. I've realized that you're William, coming to life for me."

Nicholas chuckled as the elevator dinged to their floor. "If I'm William, who's Darren? You?"

Rion shook his head. "Darren is black. Or biracial, like my sister Muriel. Half black, half white. His father was a white minister of parliament that denied him, so he was raised by his mother and grandmother. Kaleb is helping me with that experience, making sure that it's authentic and not full of stereotypes and racial tropes. I want to make sure Darren's depth is beyond what people think and see about gay black men." He opened the door with his keycard.

"Wow, that's very noble of you to do that," Nick said, giving his approval. "There aren't a lot of writers that go out of their way to make sure their work is genuine. Only the great ones do that."

"Are you calling me great?" Rion asked as he put his arms around Nick's neck.

Nick grabbed his bottom and led him to the couch. "Yup. Great mind. Great compassion. Great ass."

"Yeah, well, you're not getting any ass right now. I have work to do." But Rion followed up with a kiss.

"Boooo." Nick feigned sadness. Rion kissed his mouth again. "Then let me suck your cock," Nick said in a low and husky voice.

Rion's eyes went wide. "Yeah? Unreciprocated?"

Nick nodded. "Yeah. Just let me suck your cock for a little while, then you can ask me anything."

Rion sat down on the couch and opened his legs wide, rubbing his crotch a few times slyly. Nick knelt between his legs and unzipped his zipper, pulling his hard cock out through the slit in his boxer briefs. He stroked it a few times before he licked the underside of Rion's mushroom head around the rim, making Rion moan in his throat. He opened his mouth, and put the cock head in, and sucked the pre-cum out of his slit, then slid his mouth farther down slowly.

Rion held Nick by his ears gently and guided his slow bob with a tight suction, all the way down into Rion's dark brown and curly pubic hair up to the cock head again. Rion found himself thrusting upward into Nick's mouth gently, matching his steady pace. Nick came off a few times to catch his breath and to jerk Rion's slimy, wet penis but focused on using his mouth and tongue to give him full pleasure.

Rion leaned his head back, closed his eyes, and rode the waves of his orgasm. He absentmindedly began to thrust faster, and Nick let him pound his throat until Rion breathed out, "Holy shit. I'm cumming..."

Nick felt Rion's cock head swell and began to spurt out cum, still bitter from the night before. He swallowed and then swallowed some more until there was nothing left, and then he released Rion from his mouth. He slowly came off his knees to a stand, his cock straining in his pants.

Rion sat up and said, "Take it out."

Nick smiled and zipped down his zipper. Rion reached out, but Nick slapped his hand away, making Rion laugh. He tried again, but Nick wouldn't let Rion touch him. He stood before Rion and stroked himself quickly, his fingers moving lightning-fast over his own cock. In less than a minute, Nick said, "Open your mouth."

Rion did and stuck his tongue out. Nick came closer and placed his cock head right on Rion's tongue. Instantly, he began to jizz out directly in his lover's mouth. Nick sighed with the last couple of drops, and

Rion closed his mouth and swallowed his thick cum, then pulled Nick onto the couch with him. They laid down facing each other, kissed, and held on, smirking in between with an air of affection between them.

"I'm so into you," Rion said softly.

Nick pressed their lips together in response. "Likewise. Now ask me anything. I'll tell you everything."

They laid together as Nick told him what it was like growing up the youngest of everyone in his family, about being ignored until it was time to perform at dinners, parties, and family events. "It was clear my parents were done having children when they accidentally got pregnant with me. They already had two children, a twelve-year-old boy and a ten-year-old girl. According to my aunt Lois, the story is they were on the verge of divorce when my mother got pregnant with me. They were separated but lived in the same home until I was born, and my father immediately demanded a paternity test. Surprise, I am Niles's son! He couldn't leave now and abandon a Highton male heir, so he stayed, and now they have a loveless marriage, thanks to me."

"Do you really blame yourself for that?" Rion asked.

"No," Nick replied. "But everyone else does. That's what my aunt Lois said when she was high on Vicodin on my thirteenth birthday. I am the mistake that they saw every day."

Rion ran his fingers through Nick's hair. "Oh, Nicky," he said softly. "You're not a mistake. If for no other reason, you were put on this earth for this moment right here, to be here with me."

Nicholas's heart melted. "You're so incredibly special. You know that?"

Rion smiled. "Tell me about the relationship between you and your siblings."

"Ah. Well, they were much older than me, so I didn't really have a relationship with them growing up. But they were the ones that went to war with my parents over the decision to invest my trust fund into the magazine, reminding them that I was an adult, it was my money, and I could do what I wanted. So in the last six or so years, we have developed great relationships."

"Hmmm... I wish I could interview them, too," said Rion. "So they approve of your life choices?"

"I think they approve of me making my own choices, something neither of them were able to do growing up. And both of their marriages are technically arranged."

"Damn. That sucks."

Nick talked about his relationship with his siblings, being closer to Brian than Emma just because of the male relationship. "Emma is more like a second mother to me, a better version of Madeline. Brian is a classic older brother, ignored me mostly, pushed me around and called me scrub, but also let me hang with his friends and took me to my first strip club after I turned eighteen."

Rion was lost in Nick's voice and story when Nick looked at his watch. "We should start getting ready. Parker will be on time."

"Okay. Do I put on my suit?"

Nick smiled. "You have a suit?"

"I clean up pretty nicely," Rion said smugly.

Nick kissed his lips. "I can't wait to see it." He sat up first and tapped Rion's bottom. "Come on." He stood up and took Rion's hands to pull him off the couch, too. They stood face to face, holding both hands, and kissed again.

Nick decided to be a little more forthcoming, just in case Parker said something outrageous. Which, knowing him, he would. "I should tell you one more thing. Parker is not just my investor. He's one of my best friends."

Rion raised his eyebrow. "Best friend, huh? Does he know everything about you?"

"He does."

"Hmmm... does he know about us?"

Nick smiled. "He does."

"Good to know," Rion said with a smile. "I won't sit on your lap at dinner, though."

Nick raised both Rion's hands over his head to connect them around his neck. "You can if you want to," he purred in his ear.

Rion chuckled as Nick kissed him repeatedly behind his ear. "You don't seem like someone who wants to make it for dinner."

Nick growled in his ear. "See you in thirty minutes."

Rion slid his suit jacket on as Nicholas knocked on the door. "Ready, Ree?"

"Almost. You can come in."

Nick opened the door wearing a dark blue suit, light blue shirt, and a mixture of blues in his tie. The longer middle part of his hair was slicked back, and he had shaved, so the only hair on his face was a thin, barely visible mustache that was browner than the dirty blond color of his hair.

Rion wore a gray suit with a black button-down shirt and shiny black shoes. Nick was staring at Rion, but Rion was the one who said, "Fuck, you're gorgeous."

Nick smiled and came closer. "And you are the most handsome man I've ever had the pleasure of having on my arm." Nick straightened out Rion's collar and lapels. "I have a tie for you. If you're willing to wear it."

Rion shrugged. "Ties aren't really my thing, but sure, I'll wear one tonight, for you."

Nick ran to his room, and Rion turned back around to spray his hair again, making sure his curls stayed in place. Nick returned with a gray and black diagonally striped tie and a pocket square to match. He silently took off Rion's coat and tied his tie, put his jacket back on, and arranged the pocket square.

Nick patted his chest. "Now you're ready."

Rion looked at himself in the mirror and grinned. It was definitely a nice touch. "Lead the way."

They made their way downstairs to the Heston Blumenthal dining hall five minutes after 8 p.m. "Good evening. Reservation under Highton, Chef's table."

"Right this way, Mr. Highton. Your guest has already arrived," the host told them.

They were led to a corner of the dining room that had a ridiculously large booth for three people. A man was already sitting there, shorter than either Rion or Nick, with black hair and ice-blue eyes, and a thin beard. He stood up as Nick and Rion came closer, shaking his head.

"You naughty boys, you. Couldn't keep it in your pants long enough to be on time for dinner, eh?"

Nick smiled and grabbed his friend by the arm, and Parker did the same. "Shut up." He turned to

Rion. "Rion Matthews, this is Parker Madison, my best friend from college and the investor that has saved my ass these last couple of years."

"Hm. Couldn't pass up an opportunity to make more money, now could I?" Parker winked at Nick and turned to Rion. "Well, the famous Rion. Let me get a look at you. Do a spin." Parker twirled his finger around.

Rion looked at Nick, who had a sparkle in his eye. But he slowly did a 360 for Nick's friend. When he faced Parker again, Parker was stroking his chin and nodding. "Good choice for a sexual partner, Nicholas. Very good choice."

"Wow. Okay," Rion said in disbelief.

"Oh, I'm just jostling you!" Parker said playfully and shoved Rion's chest. "Sit down, gentlemen. Let's get the inquisition started, shall we?"

Rion immediately grew worried, but Parker turned out to be more bark than bite. Despite making sexual innuendos about Nick and Rion, he was lighthearted and fun, telling Rion about ending up with a room on Nick's floor during his one year at Harvard as an exchange student from Oxford and the things they used to get themselves into, good and bad. He asked Rion simple questions about his life and didn't press too hard when Rion gave him vague answers. Rion had a feeling Parker already knew them.

No one ordered; appetizers and entrees were brought to the table one by one by the chef himself, and the wine was forever flowing, never an empty glass. After filling up on smoked, cured salmon, duck and turnip, Hereford ribeye, and blackberry tarts, they were well into the night and relaxed. Rion could see why Nick and Parker were friends. They had different personalities—Nick was more laid back, and Parker was loud and boisterous—but they complemented each other. They were like brothers with their playful banter. And Nick seemed happy having Parker and Rion in the same room.

"Come upstairs and stay for a while," Nick requested after dinner. "Unless you have something else to do tonight. Or someone."

"Well, I don't want to disturb whatever debauchery you had planned for the evening, Nicholas. Unless I'm invited." He winked at Rion and finished his fourth glass of wine.

Nick laughed as Rion asked, "Are you bisexual too, Parker?"

"Only during certain seasons and Boxing Day," Parker said amusingly, making them all laugh.

"Well, you're not invited into my bed, but you are invited to brandy," Nick said.

"You should have led with that. Tarry no further, cheers mates." He stood up and followed Nick and Rion upstairs to the penthouse.

Rion took off his tie and suit jacket and dropped them on the living room couch while Nick pulled the brandy and three glasses and placed them on the coffee table. Parker plopped down on the other side as Nick sat next to Rion. Nick poured everyone a glass, serving himself last.

Parker lifted his glass and said, "Cheers. To new beginnings and finding things you never knew you wanted."

Nick and Rion smiled at each other and clinked glasses before they all took sips. "So, what's next for the two of you?"

Nick didn't answer. Instead, he looked at Rion shyly and shrugged a bit. Rion said, "We haven't really talked about it, but I guess we go back to our regular lives. He did offer me a job, though."

"Really?" Parker exclaimed. "Doing what exactly?"

"Book reviews. And if Rion ever wants to write for me as a freelance writer, he absolutely can," Nick told Parker.

"Well. That is ... something," Parker said, more to himself than to the others.

They continued to make small talk when Nick stood up. "Gotta relieve myself. I'm leaving you two to talk about me without me around for a moment."

Rion smiled. "That's exactly what we're going to do."

Nick leaned over and kissed his lips. Then kissed him again. He caressed his cheek before he made his way down the hall to the bathroom. When the door shut, Parker spoke. "Nick is happy. It's been a long time since I've seen him this happy. And you two are definitely stunning together."

"Thank you," Rion said sincerely.

"It's just such a shame that it won't last," he said definitively.

Rion hesitated. "I mean ... we're just ... having a good time."

Parker gave him a stern look. "It's obvious that Nick is becoming entangled with you. And you are clearly smitten with him."

Rion was quiet for a moment, then asked, "Would it be so bad if we were?"

Parker waved his hand in dismissal. "You two are so different. It can't work the way that either of you envisions it."

"But why?" Rion asked earnestly.

"Well, for starters, it's obvious that you're white trash," Parker said with a straight face, and sipped his brandy.

Rion sat up in his seat and looked at him angrily but said calmly, "What did you just say?"

"Come, come now. I didn't mean it disrespectfully." Parker again waved his hand dismissively. "Your suit is cheap polyester, and your shoes are from, what, Aldo's? Nick didn't have to say anything. I smelled it on you a mile away. And more importantly, so will his family."

Rion felt the heat of embarrassment rising from his chest to his cheeks as Parker continued. "Nick is going to try to keep you around, but you can't let that happen. They will never accept you, Rion. Nicholas has come too far to finally gain the respect of his father and the tolerance of his mother. Bringing someone like you into his life will just push them further away from him. Is that what you want?"

Rion didn't answer. They heard the toilet flush, and Parker said quietly, "Think about it. You'll either be hidden from them or destroy their fragile family. Neither are good outcomes for you. Nicholas needs a life partner that will serve his best interests. You are not it."

"But Penelope is?" Rion asked bitterly.

Parker grimaced. "God no, she's ghastly. But someone of her rank in society, yes. A female someone that can give him children and carry on his bloodline. Don't push this any further, Rion, for both of your sakes."

The bathroom door opened, and Nicholas came out. Rion tried to relax in his seat, but Nick felt the tension when he sat down. "You okay?"

"Yeah, I'm just tired. Going to bed soon," Rion mumbled.

Parker cleared his throat. "Yes, well, as it turns out, I do have somewhere else to get into this evening. Or better said, a someone," Parker said, grabbing his phone. "Walk me out, Nicholas."

"Sure," Nick replied. They all stood up, and Parker shook Rion's hand. "It was wonderful to meet you, Rion. I hope not for the last time." He winked and smiled at Rion, who did not smile back.

Nick kissed Rion's cheek. "I'll be right up." Rion nodded wordlessly.

Nick didn't say anything until they got into the elevator, then he turned to Parker and towered over him. "What the fuck did you say to him?"

Parker did not back down. "I said what he needed to hear. What you need to hear, too, but you're too thick." He patted his chest roughly. "He seemed like a better listener than you, however."

Nick was pissed. "If you ruined this for me—"

His friend interrupted his threat. "Ruin *what*, exactly, Nicholas? What *exactly* is this that you're doing here?" Parker asked incredulously. Nick opened his mouth, but no words came out. "Precisely. You don't even know what you're doing. Offering him a job? Are you mad? You let this go, or you're going to crush that adorable boy in your bed. Just like you destroyed Trixie's life."

The elevator dinged at the bottom floor. "Don't bother walking me out. I've said what I needed to say," Parker said and stepped out of the elevator. Nick let the doors close in front of him.

"Fuck," he murmured to himself. He had been trying all day to convince Rion not to pull away from him, and he was sure that whatever Parker had said was going to have him running for the hills. He took a couple of deep breaths before he entered the suite.

Rion was still sitting on the couch, slouched down, sipping his brandy. Nick sat next to him, picked up his glass, and also sipped in silence.

Rion spoke first. "You know, brandy is not my thing. Whisky, or better, bourbon. That's my thing."

"Cognac for me. Villon."

"Yup. We are definitely into different things..." Rion trailed off.

They sat silently again until Nick asked, "What did he say to you?"

Rion shook his head. "Nothing that I didn't already know, Nicholas."

"I'm sorry," Nick said softly.

"Don't be sorry," Rion said. "He wasn't wrong. I am white trash. And I'll never fit into your world. It's not—"

Anger burned in Nick's chest. He turned Rion's head to face him and stopped him from talking. "You are *not* white trash, Rion Matthews. Having rough beginnings doesn't make you white trash. You've accepted the things that have happened to you, and you didn't let them stop you. Instead, you made something of yourself. Became the strong, intelligent, talented, beautiful man before me. You are not white trash."

Rion's heart melted. "Thank you."

Nick caressed his face. "I don't want to hear anything else he had to say to you. Let's go to bed," he said softly.

Rion hesitated, then said, "I don't want to have sex tonight."

Nick was disappointed, but kissed him gently on his lips. "Okay. I'll see you in the morning."

He stood up and walked away, but Rion called out, "But... can I still lay with you? Just... lay with you."

Nick's heart leaped. He nodded. "Always."

He stepped back and held his hand out. Rion took it, and together, they went into the master bedroom. They silently stripped off their clothes, down to their underwear, and got under the covers. Nick laid on his side, and Rion turned his back to him, pulling Nick's hand around his waist and squeezing him tight. They were quiet for a long time, then Rion spoke into the dark.

"Nicky?"

"Yeah, Ree?"

"I'm not going to take the job."

Nick was quiet, then said softly, "Okay."

Neither spoke again, and they silently drifted off to sleep.

*N*ick woke up to the feeling of soft hands caressing his face. He opened his eyes, and Rion was leaning on his elbow, smiling down at him. "Hi."

"Hi," Nick said back. He reached his hand up and touched Rion's face.

"I love your morning stubble," Rion said dreamily.

"Yeah? You should see me in the wintertime. I go full-on bear," he mumbled.

"I took a picture of you," Rion confessed. "A couple of them, actually."

"Hmmm..." Nick looked over to see Rion's camera on the bed between them. "How did I look?"

"Gentle. Sweet. Innocent."

"Will I get to see it?"

"Maybe. One day."

"Hmmm..." Nick mumbled again. He closed his eyes and rolled onto his back. Rion laid on his shoulder as Nick caressed his back. "Do you have any plans today?"

"No, I didn't make any yet. You?"

"No." He let a moment pass, then said, "Don't make plans. Stay here with me in this bed all day."

"And make love?" Rion asked with a smile.

"Or talk. Or sleep. Or watch movies. Or hold each other. Whatever you want to do."

Rion was quiet for a while. Then he kissed Nick's skin and said, "I would very much like to spend your last full day with you right here in this hotel room."

"Okay."

Nick kissed his cheek and got up first to use the bathroom, his muscled cheeks and muscular back in full view for Rion. He came out and ordered room service for breakfast, then grabbed Rion's white t-shirt and put it on. It was a little snug, but neither of them minded Nick's nipples poking out.

"I'm going to keep this."

Rion grabbed a heather gray tank top from Nick's suitcase. "I'm going to keep this, too."

Nick sat in the middle of the bed, and Rion came and knelt before him. They stared at each other, then Rion put his chin on Nick's shoulder. Nick put his arms around him. No words were needed between them. They both felt the love they currently had and the loss they were destined to feel in less than a day's time. Nick held onto Rion until the bell rang and the food came.

They ate on the bed and talked. "Your turn to be interviewed," said Nick. "Tell me what life was like growing up."

"Shitty," stated Rion. "When Roslyn wasn't clean, we were bounced around from the foster care system to different strangers that were helping her out, all from her circle of drug dealers or drug users. When she was clean, she was just a pain in the ass, trying to be all loving like we were going to forget the shit she did when she was high. Muriel's dad Maurese was around, but he was fifteen when Muriel was born, so he couldn't do much for us until he was older. He's the closest thing I had to a dad, and I can still call him if I ever need him, but I try not to bother him. He's done more than enough for us. At one point, he took us in for about two years until Roslyn got clean, and it was the best and most stable period of my life. Then she fought him like hell to get us all back, only to start using again a year later. Muriel had already moved out with two kids and a boyfriend, and Ava had run away a long time ago, so it was just me and Gabby at fifteen and sixteen by that time. So we kept it quiet and managed her so we wouldn't be split up again. We've been doing it ever since."

"But she's clean now, right?" Nick asked.

"For now," Rion replied. "But it never lasts more than a year or so. Three years was her max, and she's coming up on that, so I expect her to fuck up sometime next year like clockwork. And I get it. She had a really shitty upbringing herself. Her mother was a prostitute, and she didn't know who her father was. She saw a lot of things she shouldn't have, things were done to her that shouldn't have been done, and she uses drugs to cope. She had Muriel when she was just a kid herself at fourteen. She doesn't know how to be a mom because she never really had one herself. But none of that helps the feeling of disdain I have for her."

Nick looked at him sadly. "I can't imagine."

"It's cool." Rion brushed it off. "We had each other, and that's what counts. I'd do anything for my sisters, and they'd do anything for me. They pulled together to make sure I went to college, even if it was just for two years, and moved to San Francisco with me. And with my first publishing check, I got Muriel a car so she could get around with my nephews and niece, and helped put Gabby into a better apartment for her and my niece. We'll always have each other's back."

"I wish I was close to my siblings like that growing up," said Nick. "The first time they showed the slightest bit of interest in me was to argue with my parents over my trust fund."

"Rich people problems," Rion said with a smile.

Nick chuckled. "Come here."

He held his hands out, and Rion crawled into them. They kissed softly; then Rion turned around, sat between Nick's legs, and let Nick feed him with his fingers. "We're so different," Nick said. "Lived such different lives, been through different hardships, and yet I feel like I get you. And I feel like you get me."

"That's because we have experienced the same emotions," Rion told him. "Feeling abandoned by parents that weren't physically or emotionally present. Dealing with internal unhappiness. Having to put on a face for everyone out there, but crying on the inside."

"I don't cry about it," Nick said.

"Neither do I. No point in that," Rion responded. "And that's what I mean. We get it. We just gotta keep moving, do the things that bring us joy, because we aren't going to find it anywhere else."

"The magazine does make me happy," confessed Nick. "It's not just to piss off my parents. Being my own boss, being respected by employees, actually putting out quality work, and researching real stories and articles—all of that makes me happy. I love the work that I do. It's real journalism. We're just not the New York Times."

Rion caressed his arm. "I'm proud of you, Nicky. If no one else is, just know you have one person out there that is proud of you and the work that you're doing."

Nick leaned over and kissed his cheek. "I'm proud of you, too. I don't know how thankful your siblings are for how you've taken care of them, but I'm proud that you have stepped up and become the man in your family."

Rion looked up, and they kissed softly. "I think I want to have sex now."

Nick smiled. "Well, I'm not ready yet," he said. Nick wanted to show Rion that he wanted more than just sex from him. "I just want to spend some time with you. Is that okay?"

Rion kissed him again. "Okay."

They moved to the living room and watched a movie with Rion lying in front of Nick and Nick with his arm draped over him. Rion laced their hands and moved them to his chest. About an hour into the movie, Nick heard a light snore escape from him. He looked down at Rion's sleeping face, a look of peace and serenity on it. Nick brushed his nose in Rion's curls and breathed deeply, never wanting to forget his scent. He closed his eyes and found himself drifting to sleep, also feeling comforted in the arms of the stranger from the plane.

Rion woke up first, feeling Nick's snores against his back. The room was dark, with nothing but the television to light up the shadows. Rion turned his body slowly to face Nick, but the change in his comfort led him to wake up as well. Nick opened his eyes, and stared into Rion's brown ones, then closed them again.

Rion kissed his nose. "Hi, Nicky."

Nick smiled. "Hi, Ree." He kissed his nose. "You're hungry?"

"I could go for a gourmet burger."

"Then a gourmet burger you shall have." Nick slid off the couch from behind him and went to the phone in the kitchen to order room service.

He came back and laid on top of Rion. Their lips quickly found each other, licking and teasing the outside of their mouths before Rion took the plunge first, forcing Nick's mouth open and licking the inside of his mouth aggressively. Nick opened his mouth wider and trapped Rion's tongue between his lips, sucking it first before returning to the tongue match in Rion's mouth. Their groins pushed together like swords, also fighting for dominance, but since Nicky was on top, he controlled the slow grind against Rion. They continued to make out like teenagers until their lips hurt and the doorbell rang.

"Uuuugh," Rion moaned.

Nick kissed his face. "Let's eat first. We haven't eaten since this morning."

Rion nodded as Nick climbed off him, the thin fabric of his underwear unable to hold the straining of his cock, Rion's underwear sporting a large wet spot of pre-cum. He opened the door and let the attendant bring the cart all the way to the terrace. Rion moved to the table, and they ate together.

"What's the first thing you're going to do when you get back?" Rion asked.

"Sleep," Nick replied. "The time change and jet lag are going to kick my ass. And then get a large New York pie from a local pizza shop on the upper east side. Nothing like it. You?"

"Aside from Burger King?" said Rion. "Truffle fries. Nothing like it." Nick laughed. "I'm actually going to start putting this story down on paper tomorrow. After you leave."

"At Kaleb's?"

"Nah. I'll stay here," Rion said without looking at him. "Might as well enjoy it while it lasts, living like the rich do."

Nick looked over at him and smiled, then drank some more wine. "Can I at least keep in touch with you? Call or text once in a while? Be friends?"

"You sure that's a good idea, Nicky? You might get the urge to jump on a plane and end up in San Francisco," Rion teased.

"So a clean break would be better?"

"It's for the best," Rion said casually.

"Yeah. For the best." He and Rion stared at each other. "Will you hold me tonight?" Nick asked softly.

"Tonight and every night that you'll let me," Rion responded softly.

Nick smiled. "That doesn't sound like a clean break at all."

Rion did not smile back. He stood up and came over to him. Nick moved his chair out from under the table, and Rion sat in his lap, facing him. Rion put his hands around his neck and asked, "Is that what you want? A clean break from me?"

"No," Nick admitted. "But it's for the best. Otherwise...."

Nick didn't finish his sentence, but he didn't have to. Rion knew. "Otherwise, we'd be fighting a losing battle to stay together," Rion finished for him.

"But it would be hot and passionate at first, exciting and adventurous," Nick said, holding onto Rion's butt cheeks.

"We'd fall in love. Madly, deeply, ridiculously in love with each other," Rion said with a kiss on Nick's neck.

"We'd never get enough of wanting to spend all our time together." Nick ran his hands up and down Rion's back. "We'd make promises of forever. Us against the world."

Rion sighed, still on Nick's neck. "Then one of us would get frustrated with not seeing each other enough, not being near each other."

"And our families would start to get in our ears and minds. 'Just let it go,' they'd say. 'You deserve better than what he's giving you.'"

"And we wouldn't listen at first," Rion said, holding onto Nick's neck tighter. "We'd fight hard for it."

"Until it became unbearable. And we would end up arguing all the time about dumb things."

"We'd accuse each other of being unfaithful. We'd fall into temptation and actually become unfaithful."

"It would all come out, and we'd fight terribly and say nasty things to each other," Nick said sadly.

"And it would end, badly. We wouldn't even be able to maintain a friendship after that. After all the years we had spent loving each other," Rion said just as sadly, lifting his head up from Nick's neck. "You'll be my greatest love and my biggest regret."

"You'll be the one that got away," Nick said back to him.

Rion stared at him. "It's for the best," he whispered.

Nick nodded. "I'm ready to make love now, Ree."

Rion nodded back. "Yes, please."

They kissed softly again, and then Nick stood up, taking Rion with him. "Shit, I did not know you were this strong," Rion said, wrapping his legs around his waist.

"I'm not, and you're heavy," he said, making Rion laugh.

But he walked Rion to the master bathroom before he set him down. Nick pulled Rion into the shower first. They took their time, washing each other in silence, getting in between all their creases and areas, kissing and touching along the way, both of their cocks rock solid.

Rion reached over and squeezed Nick's bottom. "You ever been fucked, Nicholas?" he asked plainly.

Nick's face immediately went red. "No. And I'm not about to be today."

Rion chuckled. "Okay. No pressure."

Nick's eyes went wide. "You're a switch?" Rion nodded with a wink. "I had no idea. With your pen name, Ryan D. Ryder, I just assume that's all you do. And the way you bent over and opened up for me that first day..."

"Well, I *really* wanted you to fuck me, so it was a no-brainer."

Nick laughed out loud. "And now you want to fuck me?"

Rion shook his head back and forth. "Yes." Nick laughed loudly again. Rion smiled and then got serious. "No, not if you've never done it. It was just a question that I had in my mind and never got the nerve to ask."

"Well, if I ever get the urge to be a bottom, you're the first person I'll call. I swear on it."

Rion smiled and gave his lover a passionate kiss. "Deal," he breathed on his lips.

They came out of the shower and fell into bed together, kissing and touching, taking their time worshiping each other's body parts. Nick started it, putting Rion's big toe in his mouth and sucking it, licking between his toes, kissing the bottom of his feet.

Rion started giggling. "I'm ticklish!"

Nick began to kiss up his thighs, but when he made it to Rion's genitals, Rion quickly sat up and pushed him onto his back. He began to kiss down his torso, little bites here and there, and put Nick's penis in his mouth, making Nick groan. But Rion only sucked a few times before replacing his mouth with his hand and moving his mouth lower. He kissed and sucked each testicle, and Nick moaned loudly. He gently lifted one leg up and licked Nick's taint.

"Uuuuugh fuck, Rion," Nick moaned.

Rion licked his finger and played with the outside, making Nick moan again. "May I?" he asked softly.

"Yeeessss..." he moaned out.

"Turn around," Rion commanded, and Nick flipped his leg over Rion's head until he was flat on his belly.

Rion took his time to not scare him too much, kissing his entire bottom softly, with gentle nibbles, before he spread Nicholas's hairy cheeks and licked his fissure. Nick tried to relax and not tense up every time Rion's wet tongue dug a little deeper into his crack. When it finally reached into his hole, Nick moaned, and his body jerked in Rion's hands. Rion pulled back just enough and used the pad of his thumb to circle the abyss a few times before spitting and digging the tip of his tongue through the ring.

"Oh my God... Rion..." Nick murmured.

"Want me to stop?" Rion asked with his face in Nick's ass.

"God no... this feels... incredible."

Rion pushed his tongue deeper, alternating between one finger and tongue, driving Nick crazy with pleasure. "You ever had your prostate touched?" Rion asked him softly.

"Fuck, Rion... What are you doing to me?"

"Can I touch it?" Rion asked instead of answering his question. "Just let me touch it." Rion added a second finger and said, "Please, Nicky. Let me touch it." He pulled his fingers out, bent down, and licked his hole again and again. "Let me touch it."

"Fuck, just touch it already!" Nick almost yelled at him.

Rion added lube to his two fingers and reinserted them into Nick's anus. Nick moaned loudly. He had had anal play before, usually with a woman, but it was nothing like this, where it was an intentional finger thrusting and reaching for his prostate. He lost himself in the feeling and found himself calling out Rion's name over and over again. When Rion's fingertips brushed against his hump, he let out a loud groan, electricity shooting from to the tip of his cock, and a spurt of pre-cum slid out.

Rion did it again and again. "Holy fuck, holy fuck," Nick moaned out.

Suddenly, Rion pulled his hands out, and Nick had never felt so empty in his life. The next thing he felt was Rion's very hard cock moving up and down his crack. Nick gasped as Rion leaned over and left a wet kiss on the back of his neck.

"I changed my mind. I want to fuck you so bad," he whispered and kissed his neck again.

"I like this domineering side of you, Rion," Nick said with a chuckle. "Almost makes me want to give up my anal virginity to you. Almost."

Rion laughed. Nick flipped over and threw him off his back, making Rion laugh harder. He got on top, kissed Nick's lips, and said, "Later, I'll let you bring me to the brink, but right now, I need to be deep inside of you. Please?"

Rion responded by lifting his legs and wrapping them around Nick's back, then moved his waist back and forth, coating his hole with Nick's dripping pre-cum. Nick's eyes went wide. "Fuck, you're dangerous."

Rion laughed and reached over to the nightstand and handed him a condom. Nick sat back on his heels and put the condom on. Rion handed him the lube, and he coated Rion inside and out, then leaned back over, and they resumed the position, with Rion's legs wide and open. Nick slid inside his happy place, gently watching Rion's face contort, then relax, as he moved out halfway, then slid back in. Rion held onto the side of Nick's ribs, closed his eyes, and moaned softly with every thrust. Nick watched him as they made love, wanting to pleasure him to the max. He switched up his movements, slow, steady, circular, faster, harder, then back to slow and steady again.

Rion reached between them and began to stroke himself. Nick continued to keep a steady pace as he watched Rion's curls mat to his forehead, his face turning pink, his body trembling beneath him. He watched Rion's mouth quiver right before he moaned out his orgasm, and strings of cum began flying out of his cock. The sight of Rion's climax was enough to make his own orgasm roll through his body quickly, and he instantly began to cum.

Rion let go of his own cock and squeezed Nick's muscled buns as he came. Nick slid out and collapsed on the side of him. "That was incredible," he said breathlessly.

"You are incredible," Rion said, moving over to him and putting his head on Nick's shoulder. "You're an incredible lover. I've never felt anything like it before."

Nick smiled and kissed his face. "It's because of you, Rion. I'm only incredible because it's you."

Rion moved closer, and they laid silent for a while, wide awake and comfortable. He broke the silence by asking, "Tell me about the last time you were in love."

Nick turned to him and touched his face. "You mean besides right now?"

Rion smiled. "Stop it."

Nick laughed. But then he told him about Beatrice. "Trixie. She was my girlfriend for most of college. I thought she was the one. I know she was the one," he said sadly.

"What happened?"

"Madeline," Nick said with a sigh. "Trixie was from Montana, came from nothing, literally dirt poor. She grew up on a farm with six brothers and sisters, and she was somewhere in the middle. Her family owned a produce market where they would sell their own fruit, vegetables, and fresh meat, and they worked hard to send her to Harvard. My mother didn't want us together. She was way outside of my world, and Madeline didn't think Trixie was pretty enough that people wouldn't care. Trixie was a mousy, glasses-wearing brunette and the most beautiful girl in the world to me. Madeline said I didn't need a smart girl. I needed a girl that would do what she was told. 'Smart girls don't do what they're told; pretty girls do so they can keep their status,' she said. I told her to fuck off with that. That I loved Trixie and I was going to marry and have a bunch of farm bred children with her. So my mother ruined us."

"What did she do?"

"First, she had a conversation with Trixie behind my back, basically telling her all the things that were wrong with her and threatening her to make her go away. Then my father offered her money to go away. When Trixie told me, I did the most logical thing, I asked her to marry me in front of the whole school our junior year."

"I'm sure that pissed them off."

"Yeah, it did. They threatened to take away my trust fund if I married her. I didn't care. I was willing to move to Montana and be a farmer. That's how much I loved her."

Rion giggled. "Now *that* I would have loved to see."

Nick smiled, but then his smile faded as he continued, "And when that didn't work, they tried to destroy her family's livelihood."

"What!? How!?"

"My father brought the building that housed their produce market and raised the rent astronomically. Within two months, he sent an eviction notice to them, then took her parents to court, drowning them financially. My mother told her the only way it would stop was if she agreed not to marry me. So Trixie ended it with me."

"Holy, holy shit. Nicholas!" Rion was outraged for him.

"Yup," he said sadly. "Her parents convinced her to end it with me, and my parents immediately dropped the suit. I tried for six months to get her back. But she was afraid that my parents would do something worse, and rightfully so. Eventually, I had to let her go."

"I'm so sorry, Nicholas. Madeline is cruel."

"Madeline is a bitch," Nick said viscerally. "I didn't talk to her for a year, either of them. When I turned twenty-one, I signed the papers for my trust fund and didn't move back home after college. I moved to the city instead, and we launched Deep Strokez Publications. They were pissed, but Emma and Brian basically told them that they ruined my life with what they did to Trixie, so they had no right to try to control what I did with my money."

"Wow." Rion was silent but then asked the question on his mind. "So if you were to show up with a man on your arm, with me, would Madeline try to destroy me?"

Nick sighed. "The truth? Yes, she would. She would dig up your past and find a reason to pull us apart. It's the main reason I haven't been in a relationship since Trixie."

"Aren't you in a relationship with Penny?" Rion asked with an eyebrow raised.

"Oh, well. Technically. Penelope is the daughter of a family friend that they have been pushing on me since we were young and ran in the same circle. One night we came together at an event, and one thing led to another. Within a week, she had told everyone that we were an item. I tried to deny it, but Emma convinced me there was no harm in giving it a shot, so I did."

"So, what's wrong with Penny?"

"Honestly? Nothing. She's smart, she's logical, she's beautiful, she's rich, a little high maintenance, and exactly the type of woman my parents approve of. She'll make a good wife someday."

"But?"

"I don't love her," Nick said plainly. "She doesn't excite me in or out the bed. She doesn't challenge me unless it challenges her status, then she becomes unbearable. I really did try the first year, but I just couldn't. I tried to break up with her, and she went to my mother in tears. My father told me that because of what I do, being with Penny is good for my image. Having a respectable philanthropist by my side. That it doesn't matter that I don't love her, only insignificant people marry for love. That I needed to do what was good for me, not what I wanted to do. He didn't say it in a cruel way, like my mother would have. My father is a very practical man, and he gave me practical advice."

"So you stayed together," Rion stated.

Nick nodded slowly. "We see each other once a month; Zoey arranges the schedule. Penny's organization is in Buffalo, and she goes back and forth to Toronto a lot. We have dinner, boring sex, and then we go back to our lives. We come together for public events, smile for our families, and again, go back to our lives. I know she doesn't love me either, but she's satisfied with what we have. It's the Highton name she wants, not me."

"So, are you going to marry her?" Rion asked.

Nick looked him in the eyes. "I don't think I can." He ran his fingers through Rion's curls softly. "Now I know I can't. Now that I know what else is out there. I have to end it. For good this time."

"Don't end it because of me," Rion said gently.

"I'm ending it because of me. I should have ended it a long time ago. It's time." Rion nodded. Nick turned it around on him. "Now tell me about your ex. The one you're not over."

Rion leaned back and looked at the ceiling. "What makes you think I'm not over him?"

Nick reached across his abs and gently caressed them. "Call it intuition."

Rion smiled while looking up. "I am over him. I am … eighty-five percent over him. Before this week with you, I was at sixty percent, so I think I'm moving in the right direction."

"How long were you together?"

"Technically, three years, but we've been on and off these last eight months. Right now, we're off. Jason is beautiful and loving, and possessive. And I need my space. I need to breathe and think and be myself. A partner should be your peace, and I am his, but he's not mine. He's my anchor, holding me in place. I thought that's what I wanted when we first met, someone to ground me, a dominating personality. But a year in, I realized what I got was a father figure, and I did not want that. I want to be attached, not caged. I'm a dreamer, Nick. I write stories for a living. I want to travel and visit faraway places, meet people, eat exotic foods, and create stories from my experiences. He's ... practical. He works in a bank making good money. He's lived in San Fran his whole life, eats the same meals every day, does the same things, and sleeps with the same four people. He doesn't stray from his routine. But he's a great guy ... and I still love him. I just don't want to be with him. I still care about him, so it's hard to let go."

Nick nodded in understanding. Rion turned to look into Nick's blue eyes. "But I have to tell you, I haven't thought about him once since I've been here, except for when you first told me about Penny and you asked if I understood complicated. I understand complicated. But now that I know what else is out there, it will be easier for me to let him go."

"Don't let him go because of me," Nick said gently, still touching his torso.

Rion repeated Nick's words. "I'm letting him go because of me. Because I can't give him what he needs. And what he's offering me, I don't want."

"What do you want?" Nick asked, moving closer to him, putting his leg over Rion's, and moving his cock against his thigh.

Rion turned his body toward Nick. "I want to make you cum again."

"Yeah, how do you want to do that?" Nick asked softly.

"Can I milk you?" Rion whispered.

Nick grinned. "Okay."

Rion's eyes went wide. "For real?"

Nick laughed. "Yeah. I told you I'd let you bring me to the brink afterward, didn't I? I keep my word."

"God, I'm so horny thinking about putting my fingers in that tight ass again," Rion said in a low, husky voice.

"Well, don't tease me," Nick said back, just as huskily. "I've been thinking about it since you removed your fingers from inside of me."

"Jesus," Rion murmured. "Turn around for me, baby."

"Baby, huh?" Nick said with a smile and turned onto his stomach.

Rion didn't answer. Instead, he grabbed the lube from between the sheets and sat on Nick's thighs. He squeezed and massaged his cheeks first, then he added lube to two fingers and gently inserted them inside. Nick was open from when he did it about an hour ago, so Rion entered a third finger.

"Holy, holy shit," Nick groaned, using Rion's catchphrase.

Rion leaned down over him, keeping his fingers inside of Nick, his hard cock rubbing against his left leg as he moved up and down against him. He alternated between two and three fingers, adding more lube until his tunnel was nice and moist.

"Tell me how it feels," Rion breathed into his neck. "Tell me."

"Pain ... and pleasure ... at the same time..." Nick breathed out. Rion switched back to his index and middle finger and found his nub again. "Hmmm... Fuck, that feels ... fuck..."

Nick's penis was rock hard against the mattress. He stretched his arms out and surrendered to Rion's fingers and his dirty talk. "You like that, Nicky? You like having my fingers inside of you? Want my tongue inside of you again? What about my cock? Wanna feel my cock in you?"

Between the feelings of Rion's fingers inside of him massaging his prostate, Rion's hard cock against the uppermost part of his thigh, and Rion's body pressing his body between his abs and bed, it was too much for him to handle. His orgasm crashed upon him, and he fell weightlessly into it. Sounds that he didn't know he could make came out of him, gargled and higher than his normal voice, as his cock began to jizz ropes of cum onto the bed. Rion must have sensed it because he moaned too, and Nick felt Rion's cum spurt against his thighs, balls, and left butt cheek.

Rion stopped moving and slid his fingers out slowly. He crawled up onto Nick's back and said, "That was the best non-anal sex I've ever had."

Nick laughed out loud. "God, I'm gonna miss you. I don't think I want to get on the plane tomorrow."

Rion kissed his neck and said, "But you have to. It's for the best."

Nick sighed. "Yeah. A clean break."

Rion slid off Nick's back, and pulled him close. They kissed for a while, stared into each other's eyes, kissed some more, then stared again.

Rion said, "Close your eyes, Nicky. I'll be here in the morning. Promise."

Nick slowly closed his eyes and fell into a dreamless sleep.

*N*ick woke up before the sun had risen and laid there in silence. Rion was laid sideways across his arm, his face in Nick's chest, his hand resting across Nick's thighs. His breathing was almost soundless, but Nick heard it, anyway. Nick didn't move at all. he laid there feeling the numbness of his hand, and Rion's breath on his skin. He wished time could stop and he could stay in that room with Rion forever. But the sun began to rise, and Rion began to stir. Nick closed his eyes and pretended to be asleep as he felt Rion roll over. He rose and went to the bathroom, giving Nick the opportunity to turn on his back and flex his hand a few times.

"It's for the best," he murmured to himself.

Rion came out and met Nick's eyes. He came over and laid on top of his chest. Nick rubbed his back, and they stayed close for another hour silently. Nick reluctantly said, "I have to get ready."

"I know," Rion replied, but he didn't move. And Nick didn't move him either.

Another thirty minutes passed. Nick glanced at the time, knowing that if he didn't rise soon, he would miss his flight.

"Rion," Nick said his name softly.

He felt Rion's chest rise deeply and fall against him heavily. He slowly slid up and off Nick's chest, and gave Nick a brave smile. "Let's take a bath together," Rion suggested.

He climbed off the bed again to go into the bathroom, and Nick followed him. Rion sat at the edge of the huge tub and made the water almost scalding hot before adding bubbles to it. He stood up and motioned for Nick to get in first. Once Nick was settled, Rion grabbed a washcloth and also entered the tub, then kneeled in front of him. He dipped it in the water and started at Nick's face, rubbing it in the corners of his eyes, inside and behind his ears, and in the creases in his neck. Rion took his time, trailing it down Nick's body, lifting his left arm and getting into the pits, scrubbing down to his hand and getting in between his fingers. Rion brought the cloth into the water and gently washed his penis, which was semi-hard, went to his groin, and washed behind his balls. Nick lifted up one leg so Rion could scrub his crack, too. Rion moved farther down the tub, washing Nick's left leg down to his foot and took his time scrubbing from heel to toes, then switched to the other foot, and did the same, coming back up on his right side of the body, repeating the process.

"Move up," he told Nick.

When Nick moved up, Rion crawled behind him, and stretched his legs on either side of him. Rion scrubbed his neck and down his back. When he was done, he put the cloth to the side and leaned back, taking Nick with him. He wrapped his arms around Nick's torso, and Nick held both of his hands underwater.

"No one has ever done that for me," Nick said softly.

"You mean the royal penis has never been cleaned, your highness?"

Nick laughed out loud. "What?"

"You've never seen *Coming to America* with Eddie Murphy?"

"No. I haven't had the pleasure."

"It's an '80s classic. You should check it out."

"Maybe I will," Nick said. They were quiet until Nick said, "I can clean you next if you want."

"Nah. I'll take a shower when I get back. I'm going with you to the airport."

"Okay." Nick let a moment pass, then said, "We have to get going then."

"I know." Rion squeezed him one time and then tapped his shoulder.

Nick stood up first, and Rion walked out of the tub behind him, grabbed a towel, and began to dry Nick's body, taking his time and feeling every muscle and bone from his neck to his feet. He wrapped the towel around Nick's midsection.

"You're gonna dress me next?" Nick asked, amused.

"I can, but I'm bad at putting on ties," Rion joked.

"Well, good thing I'm not wearing a tie," Nick responded.

He let Rion lead him to the bedroom and sit him on the edge of the bed. Rion slid down on his knees and said, "Let me suck your cock. Unreciprocated."

"I will never say no to that," Nick said, running his hands through Rion's curly hair.

Rion pulled Nick's towel off and wasted no time, grabbing hold of his cock and stroking it. He took his time, opening up his jaw and taking all of him in, up, then down again. "Fuck, you really are good at this," Nick said breathlessly, still caressing his hair.

Rion didn't respond, concentrating on giving Nick a slow and meaningful blow job, sucking, licking, and stroking. Nick closed his eyes and moved his waist around, coating the roof of Rion's mouth with his steady flow of pre-cum, moaning loudly, freely, appreciatively at Rion's tongue. All too soon, he began to feel his climax. He tried to slow it down, but Rion's suction was like a vice grip on his cock. Without warning he exploded, and Rion sucked every drop out of him, leaving Nick's piss-slit clean and his cock head glistening wet.

Rion sat back and closed his eyes. Nick started to ask, "You want me to—"

"No," Rion said firmly. "You need to get dressed and get ready to go. So go."

"I have some time," Nick said, knowing he really didn't.

"Get dressed, Nicholas. It's time to go," Rion said, void of emotion.

Nick stood up and looked at Rion, still sitting there with his hands in his lap. His eyes were closed, his cock semi-hard. He leaned over and kissed Rion's forehead, then began to get ready. Nick went into the bathroom to grab his toiletries, and when he came out, Rion wasn't on the floor anymore. He packed his carry-on and made sure he didn't leave anything, then he reached back into his bag and pulled out his red shirt, the shirt he had worn to London six days ago. He folded it and left it on the bed.

"It's for the best," he whispered to himself and dragged his suitcase out of the bedroom.

He found Rion at the front door, fully dressed and scrolling through his phone. "I called the car service. They're already waiting out front. You ready?" Rion asked without looking at him. "You have less than three hours to make your flight."

"I'll make it," Nick said confidently.

Rion nodded. He glanced at Nick and said, "Let's go."

Nick followed him out the door and toward the elevator. Nick got on first, and Rion behind him. When the doors closed, they both stared straight ahead. Nick reached over gently and touched his fingertips. Rion allowed it, then held his hand fully, lacing their fingers together. Rion held on and led him out of the hotel past the front desk, not giving Nick the opportunity to formally check out. At the taxi, Nick put his suitcase in the trunk and followed Rion into the car with his laptop bag. The car took off, heading to Heathrow.

At first, they sat apart, then Rion moved closer, putting his head on Nick's shoulder. Nick touched Rion's thigh. They were silent for most of the ride, and then Rion spoke.

"Nicky? Why weren't you sitting in first class? Why were you at the back of the plane like me?"

"I stopped riding first class years ago," he said. "The people in first class are boring and sometimes pretentious. They don't want to talk. They just want to be left alone. I like having conversations with strangers on planes."

"Me, too. I'm always starting conversations with strangers."

"Best decision I ever made, to sit near you."

Rion reached his hand over and touched Nick's. "I'm going to miss you."

"Me, too, Ree. Me, too." He flipped his hand over and held Rion's back.

When they got to the airport, they both exited the vehicle, but Rion stayed between the open car door. Nick grabbed his bag and rolled it onto the sidewalk. Rion walked over to him and they hugged tightly.

"Goodbye, Rion."

"Goodbye, Nicholas."

Nick gave him a peck and let go. Rion moved back to the car door and watched Nick walk a few steps, trying not to let his face show what he felt on the inside. Suddenly Nick turned around and dropped his bags, the handle of the suitcase hitting the concrete with a loud clang. He walked quickly up to Rion and grabbed his face, pushing their lips together forcefully. Rion reached up and held onto Nick's neck, opened his mouth, and let Nick tongue him aggressively. They stood in front of the airport in the bright morning sun, letting their intense kiss speak their feelings for each other. The minutes lasted forever, their lips and tongues never getting enough. Rion knew if he did not stop it, Nick would not get on the plane. And he knew Nick had to go.

Rion pulled back slightly out of the kiss and leaned into Nick's neck. "Nicky," he murmured.

Nick held Rion's face back up and kissed him one last time. His eyes searched Rion's face, and he kissed him again, one last time. Then he turned around just as abruptly as he did before, picked up his bags, and walked into Heathrow Airport without a glance back, leaving Rion's heart outside his chest.

Nick checked in, chose his seat at the kiosk, and went right to the gate that was just starting to board. He went down the aisle to his seat, 19B, and sat down. He looked over at 19A and smiled. An older woman occupied the window seat, and she smiled back at him.

"Business or pleasure?" she asked him first.

He told her, "Business at first. But it became ... life changing. So pleasure, too. I'm heading home."

"That's lovely. Pleasure for me, I met my grand-niece. I'm also heading home."

"How fun. I'm glad you got a chance to do that."

"Thank you. And I'm glad your business trip turned out pleasurable."

"It was, thank you."

He leaned back and closed his eyes, spending the flight reliving every single moment he had spent during the last six days with the stranger from the plane.

Rion sat at the table typing furiously. He knew what time the plane landed but didn't know how long it would take Nick to get home. He glanced at the clock every twenty minutes or so, but continued to focus on Darren and William's first meeting during freshman orientation at the University of Oxford and how they quickly connected, only to find out that they were roommates. His feelings were mixed. He wanted Nicholas to call and let him know he was home. But he didn't want Nicholas to call because that would not be a clean break, not what they had agreed upon. He wasn't sure which option would kill him faster.

He dug deeper into his story, focusing on his characters' love lives instead of his own. When his phone finally buzzed next to him, it startled him and he flinched. He grabbed it quickly. It was a text from Nick.

[Nick: cheeseburgerandfries.png]

Rion found himself laughing uncontrollably. When he got himself together, he sent a text back.

[Rion: Good, huh?]

[Nick: I will never judge your choices again.]

[Rion: LOL]

[Nick: I miss your laugh.]

[Rion: Dammit, Nicky. If this is your idea of a clean break, you suck at it.]

[Nick: I can't help it. NWAWR]

It took Rion less than a moment to figure out what the acronym was, and his heart immediately melted.

[Rion replied back: RWAWN2]

[Nick: I'll dream about you tonight.]

[Rion: And every night for a while.]

[Nick: I'm lying here already missing the way your body feels next to me.]

[Rion: Inside of me. I miss you inside of me.]

[Nick: Fuck. This is not a clean break.]

[Rion: We are so incredibly fucked aren't we?]

[Nick: I almost turned back around and got on the next plane to Heathrow when I landed in New York. That's how fucked we are.]

[Rion: Don't do that. If I see you, I won't stop myself from falling for you this time. Don't do that to me.]

[Nick: Can I call you at least? Can I hear your voice?]

Rion held the phone tighter in his hand, knowing he should say no. Instead, he pressed the phone icon next to Nick's name. Nick answered the phone on the first ring.

"Ree," he said softly.

"Hi, Nicky," Rion said softly back. Neither spoke for another minute, letting the longing in the silence speak volumes. "What are you doing?"

"Lying on my couch looking up at the moon," Nick said. "It makes me feel closer to you, knowing you can see it, too."

Rion stood up and went over to the terrace. "It is the same moon, isn't it?"

"The very same." Nick let out an audible sigh. "You're gonna be okay?"

"No," Rion replied. "But I will be, eventually."

"Yeah. Me too." They were silent for another long moment, and then Nick said, "Get some rest. It's after midnight over there."

Rion realized he had not eaten all day. "I will in a moment. After I order my gourmet burger and pretend like it's a Whopper." Nick chuckled. "Will you call me tomorrow?"

"Yes," Nick said automatically. "And every day you'll let me."

"Okay," Rion agreed. "Call me tomorrow. We'll figure out the day after that."

Nick smiled into the phone. "Deal. Good night, Rion."

"Good night, Nick." Silence enveloped them again until Rion pressed the End button first, knowing Nicky never would have.

Nicholas called Rion every day when he woke up for the rest of the week, and since it was almost noon in the UK, he was either out and about taking more pictures or sitting outside at a restaurant writing his manuscript. They spoke until Nick had to go to work. Then Rion would call Nick before he went to bed every night until the moon rose for Nick. They would stare at it as they talked about Nick's workday, what stories and articles *Deep Strokez* was considering, how his staff took the news of going online completely, coming up with marketing ideas. And when they hung up, Nick would remind Rion with a text:

[NWAWR]

Rion's phone rang the following Saturday morning. "Hey, Ree Ree!"

"Jesus, Nicky, no," Rion said with his face scrunched up. "Ree is enough."

Nick laughed. "What are you doing?"

"Sitting on the floor of the balcony, typing. What are you doing?"

"I just came back from the gym downstairs, and now I'm settled on my couch with a good book."

"Yeah? What's it about?"

"It's about a bisexual man who cheated on his husband and is trying to avoid his feelings of guilt, so he ends up sleeping with women again, something they agreed upon when they got together."

Rion sat up and gasped. "How did you find my book!? It's only sold in certain places."

Nick chuckled. "You told me your name, and that's all I needed to know. I found your publisher and your bio on their website, Ryan D. Ryder. Cute avatar pic."

"Damn, you really did find me!" he said, astonished. "Well, don't hold out on me. What do you think?"

"I can't put it down, Ree," Nick said excitedly. "The suspense is killing me. Does the husband know? And if he finds out, will Greg spiral? End up back in the psych ward? This is a crazy story. I guess I thought it was going to be all about sex, but it's so much more.

I'm really trying to see how there is going to be a happy ending here."

Rion laughed. "I guess you're going to have to read on to find out."

"You're a really good writer, Ryder," Nick said.

"Well, thank you, Nicholas."

"You're also a very good *rider*, with an R, Ryder," Nick teased.

"Ugh, don't start your shenanigans," Rion groaned.

"Can't help it. I miss you. And this erotic thriller I'm reading is not helping."

"You should go out. Meet a woman and take her home. Or a him. Or a they. Forget about me."

"I'll never forget about you. And anyway, I don't ever take strangers back to my apartment."

"You took me back to your hotel room," Rion said with a smile.

"Yes, but I wouldn't have taken you back to my home. It's the first thing I bought with my inheritance money. It's my sanctuary, my safe space. The first place I've ever had that was just my own. No ties to anyone in my family."

"Yeah, yeah, I got it. We would have fucked in a back alley, no sweat."

Nick laughed. "No, I would have taken you to the Marriott Marquis in Times Square. Shown you a good time. I still can if you want." Rion was silent, and Nick knew he had said too much. "Sorry. Clean break, right?"

"It already isn't so clean, Nick. We talk every day like two people who are going to see each other again."

It was Nick's turn to pause. "Will I never see you again, Rion?"

"I don't know, Nick. I honestly do not know," Rion replied softly.

"Do you want to see me again?" Nick asked softly back.

"You know I do. But..." he trailed off.

"I know. You don't have to say it. I know." They were quiet. "I'll let you get back to writing."

"Wait... Stay for a little bit. Talk to me. Please?" Rion pleaded.

Nick sighed. "You're sending me mixed messages, Ree. You're asking me to let you go. But then you don't want me to let you go. What do you want me to do, Rion? Hold on or let go?"

"I wish I had an answer to that," Rion said sadly. "I don't mean to send you mixed messages, but I'm feeling conflicted. Our hearts want one thing when our minds are telling us something else. So what do we do?"

Nick sighed again. "Let's not dig into this right now. Let's talk about Greg and his conflicted heart. I can't believe he cheated on Beau. What an asshole."

Rion smiled. "What chapter are you up to?"

The next night, Nicholas called him. "Still going out with Kaleb and the crew tonight?" he asked.

"Yup," Rion responded. "A comedy show. Then to some bar in East London. Is it bad that I'm hoping Lennox doesn't show up?"

Nick laughed. "She still hates you?"

"Does she ever. I really took something from her that was destined to be hers."

"Now we both know that's not true," Nick said. "You were always the only one that I wanted. That I still want."

"Yeah, well, try telling her that."

"I still want you, Rion," Nick said seriously.

Rion sighed. "Nick—"

"You don't have to say it," said Nicholas. "I just need to know that you still want me as much as I want you."

"You already know the answer," said Rion. "But we can't be together. It's just going to be too hard. We agreed. It's for the best."

"I know," Nick agreed. "But I just needed to hear you say it. Say you really want me as much as I want you."

"Ree will always want Nicky, too," Rion said softly.

"That's all I need to know," Nick said softly back. "Have fun tonight. We'll talk tomorrow."

"Okay. Are you okay, Nick? You sound... I don't know."

"I'm good. Just getting my head on straight. Doing what I have to do, you know?"

"Okay, what does that mean?" Rion asked curiously.

"I'll tell you tomorrow," he said evasively. "Tell Kaleb 'hi' for me. And be nice to Lennox. She lost the greatest thing that could ever happen to her."

Rion laughed. "Tell her to be nice to me. I know she purposely spilled her drink on me last week."

Nick laughed loudly at that. "Good night, Rion."

"Night, Nicky. Dream about me, okay?"

"Every night, baby. Every single night."

Rion hung up first and smiled. Nick still brought so much joy to his life, even though they were literally an ocean apart. He called the car service to take him over to Brixton to spend his Sunday night clubbing with his English friends.

Rion's bladder woke him up before he normally would have gotten up. He groaned and made his way to the toilet, vowing to spend fewer nights drinking with Kaleb. He stumbled back to bed, needing at least two more hours of sleep, when he heard the click of the front door opening. He thought it was a fluke until he heard the door softly close. He sat up and listened and heard a noise in the hallway. Rion jumped off the bed and ran to the hallway, and then he froze.

Nick was standing there in a dark gray, zippered, Tommy Hilfiger hoodie with sweatpants to match, and a pair of gray and white Nike's on his feet, pulling his carry-on suitcase. His face was scruffy, but his eyes were clear. He stood there and stared at Rion, longing in his eyes.

"What are you doing here?" Rion said harshly. Nick opened his mouth to speak, but no sound came out. Rion's eyes went wide with fear. "No, Nicky... No."

"Rion, I—"

"No!" Rion yelled and started walking away, then walked back, waving his hands around furiously. "No... you can't ... do this..."

"Ree."

"It's never gonna work!" he yelled.

Nick sighed as Rion started pacing up and down the hallway. "This is insane... insane!" he yelled again. Nick nodded, letting him continue.

"You shouldn't have come. There is no way this is going to go anywhere. Your family will never accept me. Madeline will try to destroy me. You can't just show up with a guy on your arm and think that it's all going to work out. I've seen this story. I'm *writing* this story. They'll disown you completely. Madeline will try to destroy me. Parker was right. I'm white trash, and that's all they'll ever see. They'll think I'm after your money. I'm not going to be the reason you lose your family. And did I mention your mother will try to *destroy me*!?"

Nick continued to nod.

"And my family, fuck *all*... They'll never trust you; they'll never believe this is real. My sisters will be convinced you only want to be with me for the experience, and that eventually, you'll go back to a woman that you can marry and have babies with to carry on the Highton bloodline and legacy. One that Madeline wants for you, like Penny. They'll think you're just slumming it. Nothing that you'll ever do will be right in my sisters' eyes."

Nick nodded, and Rion continued to pace, giving him all the reasons they shouldn't be together.

"And even if all that was solved, we don't even live on the same fucking coast! How the fuck would that even work!? You're getting on a plane to come see me, what, once every two weeks? And you expect me to get on a plane every two weeks, too? How long would that even last!? Did you forget how I am on planes? I'm not getting on a plane to come see you, Nicholas!"

Rion finally stopped pacing and stood in front of him. "We're kidding ourselves if we think this is ever, ever going to work. We're too different. I don't want to get involved in your rich people problems. You don't want to get involved with someone who has a drug addict for a mother and a mentally ill sister. We can't be together. It's too hard. It's already hard! Why did you come back? We were supposed to be pulling away from each other... We can't.... It can't..."

Nick was still nodding in agreement with all of Rion's words, even after Rion trailed off and stared at him with shock and confusion in his wide brown eyes. They held eye contact until Nick said softly, "I need you, Ree."

Those four words brought all of Rion's walls down. He stopped fighting his feelings completely and walked right into Nick's chest. Rion wrapped his arms around him, then let his hands travel up his back past his shoulder blades and held on as closely as he could to Nick's body, trying to crawl into his skin if possible, breathing into his neck. Nick's arms circled his body and held him just as tight.

"I missed you, Ree," he said softly. "Did you miss me?"

"A thousand times a day," Rion said into his neck. "So what happens now, Nicholas?"

"I don't know," Nick said honestly. "I don't know what will happen when we leave here. All I know is that I need two more weeks with you. Then we'll go home."

Rion let all the air out of his lungs and let Nick hold him. "We'll leave London together? Get back on the same flight and go home?"

"Yes. It's what should have happened. We came together. We should leave together."

"Okay. Two more weeks. Then it's over," Rion said unconvincingly.

"Then it's over," Nick lied back. They held each other, then Nick said again, "I've missed you so, so much, Ree."

Rion pulled back first and stood in front of him. He unzipped the zipper of Nick's sweater, slowly, and slid it off his shoulders, touching the center of his black tank top. As soon as he did, he felt the heat coming from his body, and it immediately transferred to his own. The magnetism was back, and there was no way he was going to resist. He wordlessly reached down for Nick's hand and led him to the bedroom, leaving his suitcase in the hallway.

Once there, Rion kissed his lips softly but moved swiftly to take off his tank top. He kissed and licked Nick's neck, down to his collarbone, and leaned over to lick his perky pink nipples. He continued to travel down Nick's body, pulling his sweatpants and underwear down as he got on his knees, leaving them crumpled at Nick's ankles. He put his face in Nick's hairy crotch, his hair slightly damp from sitting on a plane for seven hours. He smelled of sweat and his natural, musky scent. Rion breathed deeply, relishing the odor of the man before him, kissed his thighs, and licked the crease at his groin before he slid his favorite piece of anatomy in his mouth, not stopping until his chin hit Nick's sweaty testicles, completely blocking his airway.

Nick groaned like a man in pain. "Uuuuuugh... God, I missed you, Rion."

Rion didn't answer, couldn't answer, because he continued to deep throat him as Nick pulled his hair and massaged his scalp. But then he pulled back from Rion's mouth and said, "I want you to know that I didn't come here for this. I just wanted to hold you. Lay with you. Sleep next to you. I just need you by my side."

Rion stood up. He took off his t-shirt and underwear swiftly and said, "And I need you inside of me. Now."

Before Nick could utter a word, Rion turned around and climbed onto the bed. He put two pillows under his stomach and laid on them, opening his legs as wide as they would go, holding his cheeks open, and leaving his pink hole completely visible. Nick gasped and grabbed his own cock, which immediately hardened. He crawled onto the bed behind him and stuck his tongue inside Rion's pucker first.

Rion's entire body jerked, making his fingers slip, but Nick caught his bottom in both of his hands and held it open, continuing to assault Rion's ass with his tongue. He used one finger, then two, to open him up, happy that his hole had gone back to its normal tightness in the week they had been apart. His cock ached to claim him once again.

Nick came off the bed and went to the top drawer of the nightstand to get the lube and condoms where they had left them. He came back behind Rion on the bed, who had not moved an inch, only his eyes following Nick's body, thirsting for the swinging meat between his thighs. Nick took his time spreading the cool gel up and down his crevice, pushed a glob inside, moved it around with two fingers, and pulled out. A part of him, a huge part, wanted to push his entire cock inside of Rion unsheathed and breed him, but he would never do so without Rion's expressed permission. So, reluctantly, he slid on the condom and added lube to it as well.

Nick lined himself up, and Rion tensed, then relaxed as Nick's cock head breached his outer ring. Rion groaned and grabbed the sheet; his body had almost forgotten how thick and long Nick's penis was. Nick paused once his cock head was in, then slid farther down until he bottomed out. He leaned over and laced one hand with Rion's, held onto his waist before he pulled all the way out, then breached him again. Rion cried out in agony and pleasure. Nick did it again, pulling all the way out, then sliding back in again until his balls rested against Rion's bottom. He continued sliding in and out, prolonging the feeling for both of them.

Rion squeezed tightly to Nick's fingers as Nick continued the deliberate strokes, feeling like he was dying every time Nick pulled out, then brought back to life when Nick filled him again, sliding against his internal nub. His cock seemed to be asking Rion over and over again, "Did you miss me when I was away?" and Rion's cries gave him the yes he needed to hear and feel.

Rion's eyes unintentionally started sprouting tears. He didn't know when was the last time he cried; probably when he was fourteen and the judge told them they had to leave Maurese's house and go back to living with Roslyn. It was like a death sentence to him. These tears were different. Rion found himself drowning in the emotional connection between them. Sex with Nick was an emotional act, almost spiritual. Nick wanted to become one with Rion, wanted him to know that his intentions were pure, his heart was open, that his body belonged to him and him only. He was grateful to be on his belly so that Nick wouldn't see the wetness on his cheeks. Rion rubbed his face into the sheets before he moved his body up into a kneeling position so that it was impossible for Nick to pull all the way out. Nick instead leaned down on him, both palms flat on the bed beside Rion's, his face in Rion's hair, his eyes closed as they moved together as one, Rion pushing back when Nick thrusted in, sliding away from each other just enough to join together again, their climax coming in like the tide.

They moaned in sync, Rion's "Aaah's" to Nick's "Ohh's," Rion's body still trembling, Nick's shivering although he was sweating profusely. Their bodies rocked and rocked and rocked until Rion saw white as his orgasm blinded him, and he let out a loud cry, his cock pumping out cum onto the sheets. His body completely seized up around Nick, giving him no choice but to cum right behind him, letting out his own cry.

Rion mumbled incoherently and stretched out onto the bed, taking Nick with him. Nick reached under his belly and pulled out the pillows, making Rion more comfortable. He didn't want to but knew he had to pull out. He did so slowly, and Rion whimpered at the emptiness. Nick leaned down to pull the condom off him, tied the end, and lazily threw it on the floor near the bed, not wanting to be away from Rion for a moment.

He turned to his side and took Rion with him, Rion's back against his chest, and reached down to pull the covers over them both. Rion laced his fingers with Nick's, kissed his knuckles, and held his hand to his chest. Within moments, they were both asleep, comfortable in each other's arms once again.

*R*ion's phone rang. "Hey, arsehole, did you fall into the Thames? Where the bloody hell have you been the last week!?" Kaleb yelled in his ear.

Nick, who was lying next to him on the couch, head to feet, smiled while working on his laptop. Kaleb was so loud he heard every word. "Tell Kaleb I said, 'Hi.'"

Rion said, "Nicholas is here. He said, 'Hi.'"

"Blimey. You should have led with that. 'My boyfriend's back, and I got no use for my mates, yeah.'" Then he yelled, "Nick, the prodigal son, returns!"

They both chuckled as Rion put the phone on speaker. "What's going on, K?" Rion asked. "What are you getting into tonight?"

"Nuthin' man, just hanging out, but next week we're having a going away gathering in your honor, yeah. Bring Nick with you. I'll be sure to keep Lennox far away from the two of ya."

Nick smiled at his computer while Rion answered him. "That sounds like fun, minus the Lennox part. I'm always up for a good party."

"Good. Nine o'clock at the Courtyard next Wednesday. I'll let you get back to whatever it is that you've been doing the last eight days."

"Later, Kaleb," Rion said and hung up. He looked over at Nick. "It would be good for us to see other people."

Nick agreed with a nod. "Seeing how we've been cocooning, I think that's a fair assessment."

It took two full days before Nick and Rion made it out of the master bedroom. They made love. They slept. They ordered room service. They watched movies. They made love some more. They spent the next couple of days exploring, hand in hand. Rion took Nick on the Underground, something Nick had never done, taking it to places like Hempstead and East Ham just to walk around. Nick got them tickets to a football match in Wembley Stadium, and they both enjoyed themselves, spending more time talking with fans than actually watching the game. Rion demanded that they visit The Blind Beggar in East End, and Nick was thoroughly impressed with its fascinating, although gruesome, history. Nick took Rion to Canvey Island for a beach day. Rion took Nick on The Blood and Tears walk. Nick made Rion get on the London Eye, which Rion hated; Rion made Nick take the Warner Brother's *Harry Potter* movies tour, which Nick hated. Rion wrote in between; Nick worked in between.

They never discussed the after; they simply enjoyed every moment. Kaleb's phone call was the first time they had paid attention to the clock winding down on their time together.

"Hey, Rion?" Nick asked without looking up. "What's your flight number?"

"Oh." Rion picked up his phone and looked at it. "American Airlines again, another red-eye, leaving on the 30th. AA 2453. That's the first one going to JFK. My second flight is... well, you don't need that info."

Nick looked up at Rion, but Rion had already gone back to writing. "Okay," Nick said casually. He went onto the website to make sure there were tickets available on the same flight and bought a one-way to JFK.

After a few minutes, Nick asked, "Wanna talk about it? About us?"

Rion sighed and didn't stop typing. After a while, he said, "No. Not yet."

"Okay, Ree." Nick decided to change the subject completely. "The rental will be here at 9 a.m. Two days in Bath at an English mansion, then two days in Dartmoor, hiking and such. We'll be back in time for the gathering at the Courtyard on Wednesday."

"Cool," Rion said, still not looking up.

"Ree?"

"Hm?"

"Look at me."

Rion kept typing, and Nick waited. Finally, he looked up. Nicholas smiled at him. Rion sighed, then smiled back.

They walked in, hand in hand, and their table immediately cheered upon seeing them. Their friends stood up one by one and hugged Rion and Nick. Lennox gave them both a tight smile and hug, and Rion heard her whisper to Nick, "I guess he's the one, innit?"

He said back to her while looking at Rion, "Yeah, he's the one." But he kissed her cheek and gave her another genuine hug.

Rion and Nick sat next to each other, just as they had the last time they were all together, but more affectionately. Finger food and wine were already on the table, so everyone immediately dug in. They reminisced about Rion's adventures in London, with Nick discussing how Rion pretended not to be wide-eyed while going through the million-dollar homes. Kaleb and Sonny talked about all the fun things they got Rion into, such as pretending to dine and dash at a Caribbean restaurant that Kaleb's uncle owned the first night they met and having Rion wash dishes in the back. They gave Rion gifts, a huge British flag, a box of expensive teas, a large picture of the Beatles on Abbey Road, and a United Kingdom–scented candle.

Rion noticed Lennox was nicer to him, joked around, and playfully touched his arm a few times. After dinner, as their group moved around to the bar and the dance floor, she leaned over and patted his leg. "I think I'm going to miss that stupid face of yours," she said with a smile.

"Does that mean you're no longer mad at me for taking Nick away from you?" he asked and smirked.

"Well, you had him first, so..." She rolled her eyes and then winked at him. "But I'm going to pretend he's mine for another hour and rub onto his muscled arse while we dance. I hope you don't mind, yeah."

Rion laughed. "Have at it. Just know that he's going home with me tonight."

"Ooooh, cheeky bastard, aren't you?" she said sarcastically, and kissed his cheek.

Nick was coming from the bar and was about to sit down when Lennox grabbed his hand. "Dance with me!"

He looked at Rion, startled, but Rion nodded as if to say, "It's fine." Nick put his beer down next to his lover and went with Lennox to the dance floor. They danced together for a couple of songs, and Rion sat watching them as he sipped his beer.

Kaleb sat down next to him and said, "Feels like déjà vu, innit?"

Rion turned to him, smiled, and held his beer up to his friend. "Cheers, mate."

"Cheers!" Kaleb said happily, and they clinked glasses.

They quietly watched the two dancing together. "How did you know?" Rion asked Kaleb, without looking at him. "Me and Nick."

"Ah. That wasn't hard if you were paying attention. It was clear there was something between you two. He looks to you for approval, what he says, where he goes, and checks in to make sure you're okay. And you move around him like you're itching to be next to him, but you hold out. Even now, you still kind of do that. Not sure why. Obviously, you're a pair."

"Because it won't last. In two days, it will be all over."

"Because that's what you both want?" Kaleb asked, turning to him fully.

"Because it can never work. Because it's for the best."

"Pffft." Kaleb scoffed. "When two people are attracted to each other like you two are, the universe will find a way to put you back together. Just watch."

Rion smiled a little. Nick looked up and saw Rion watching and winked at him. "Maybe. We'll see." Kaleb nodded.

"Hey, K," Rion said, turning to him. "Thanks for everything you've done for me this month. Not just helping me with the story, but for actually being my friend."

"You got a best mate for life over here, man. Never forget it." He reached over and gave Rion a brotherly hug.

Rilianne came over and said, "Dance with me, you American, you!" Before he could protest, she pulled him to his feet.

Rion and Nick continued to dance with others, but, at the end of the night, gravitated toward each other, Rion holding onto Nick's hips and Nick rubbing his hands up and down Rion's back. They didn't talk, just stared into each other's eyes, kissing lightly every so often, leaning into each other's shoulders. Even the faster songs had their bodies against each other.

Sonny eventually tapped Rion on the shoulder. "Looks like you have some goodbyes of your own to do, so we're off."

They hugged, and Sonny hugged Nick, too. One by one, they came over to say their goodbyes to Rion and Nick, making promises to keep in touch. Rion and Nick turned back to each other and continued to dance together. They stayed until last call, then left holding hands and walked the streets of London for a while, talking about nothing. They walked for so long that they realized they were miles from the hotel, so they hailed a taxi and jumped in.

Quietly, they made their way to the hotel and upstairs to the room. They entered the bedroom, laid on the comforter on their sides, and faced each other. Rion put his arm on Nick's hip and asked, "Why didn't you kiss me that first day?"

Nick was confused. "I did kiss you. Right after we..." He smirked.

Rion shook his head. "No. You pulled my face toward you, but you didn't kiss me. You hesitated. I kissed you."

"I didn't hesitate, I..." Nick was looking for the right words. "I wanted to make sure that you wanted to kiss me. What we did that first time wasn't exactly intimate, so I didn't know if you wanted to be that close to me. Maybe you didn't want to kiss me like I wanted to kiss you."

"I want to kiss you now," Rion said softly.

Nick leaned in and kissed his lips. "And then what?"

Rion moved into his neck and licked it first, then kissed it and said, "I want to ride your cock."

"Yeah? Ryan D. Ryder?" Nick teased. "You want to ride me?"

"If you'll let me," Rion said and sucked his neck. "May I?"

Nick leaned up and looked Rion in the eye. "Why do you always ask me for permission? 'Please' and 'May I' and all that?"

Rion smiled. "You don't like consent?"

Nick shrugged. "I just never thought of it that way. You know I want you to."

"But it's better when you tell me," Rion said. "So I know exactly how far I can take things with you. Also, consent is sexy to me. For example…" He pushed Nick onto his back. "May I take off your clothes?"

Nick smiled. "Yes."

"May I…" Rion lifted up Nick's shirt and breathed on his pecs. "Lick your nipples?"

"Fuck. Yes."

Rion dragged his tongue across Nick's left nipple, making Nick moan. He moved his tongue along his chest to the right nipple and did the same. He sat up and took off Nick's shirt completely. He trailed his tongue down his hard chest, put his tongue in Nick's belly button, and paused to unbuckle his belt. He pulled down his jeans first, then pulled down Nick's underwear, leaving his lover completely naked on the bed.

But instead of touching him, he stood at the bottom of the bed. "I want to take off my clothes. Do you want me to take off my clothes?" Rion asked softly.

Nick's eyes were wide with desire. "With all due respect, take off your fucking clothes, Rion."

Rion stifled a laugh and began to undress as Nick stroked his cock. When he was also fully naked, Rion said seductively, "I would very much like to get on top of you and grind my cock against yours. Would that be acceptable?"

Nick laughed out loud. "Jesus, Rion. Are we really doing this?"

"Tell me what you want," Rion said seriously. "Tell me exactly what will make you feel good right now."

Nick nodded. "Me, inside of you. Deep inside of you. Would *you* like that?" Rion's cock involuntarily twitched, making Nick smile. "That wasn't a verbal response."

Rion laughed and crawled up onto the bed over Nick. They kissed, and then Rion said, "I would like very much to be deep inside of you, too. It's okay to say no to that if you don't want that."

Nick looked Rion in his eyes. For the second time in his life, he considered what it would feel like to have a cock inside of him. Not just any cock, Rion's cock. Rion's seven and a half inches, thick at the mushroom head, long and angled cock. For Rion to make love to Nick the way Nick made love to him. But the fearful side of him knew he was getting caught up in the moment of their sensual and consenting foreplay.

"No. I would not like that right now. Is that okay with you?"

Rion cocked his head to the side and kissed his cheek. "Yes, I am okay with that. When you are ready, you'll let me know."

Nick pulled Rion's lips to his mouth, and they kissed aggressively. Nick pulled Rion on top of him fully. After a full minute, Nick pulled back and asked, "Can I be inside of you now?"

"Yes. But I'm the rider. Can I ride?"

"Okay, I'm done," Nick said seriously. "You have all the permission in the world to ride this cock all the way to the Kentucky Derby." He handed Rion the lube and said, "Let's go."

Rion chuckled, then handed it back to Nick. He leaned into Nick's body and enunciated each word, "I would very much like it if I get to suck your cock while you put lube on your fingers and put it into my very tight ass hole, preparing me for your thick and juicy cock inside of me. Would you like to do that?"

Nick's cock twitched underneath him. Rion smiled. "That's not a verbal response."

"You're killing me, Ree," Nick breathed out, his heart racing at the anticipation.

Rion licked Nick's lips and said, "I need you to tell me yes."

"Holy shit, yes, yes, yes!" Nick yelled.

Rion moved into position to the right of him, leaning his head over Nick's groin, and Nick sat up. Rion slid Nick's cock head into his mouth, and Nick groaned, never having a blow job feel so satisfying, realizing Rion was right; consent was sexy. He put lube onto his fingers and began to slide them up and down Rion's crack before finding his hole and digging in. Rion moaned with Nick in his mouth and slid his lips farther down. Nick moaned and added more lube to his fingers as Rion came back up to the head, then went down again.

They took their time, a slow cock suck, a slow finger thrusting, until Rion sat up first. He looked at Nick lustfully, words no longer needed. Nick moved back to the center of the bed, laid down, and put his arms behind his head. Rion moved over his body and put the condom on Nick first, then sat on his chest. He reached behind him to hold on to Nick's cock, and moved backward, penetrating himself. Once the cock head was firmly in place, Rion pressed his body downward, connecting himself to Nick's organ, until there was nothing left but the testicles at the end of his shaft. He began to move; upward, then down again, keeping eye contact with his lover, breathing hard through his mouth. Nick's grunts were in his throat. He allowed Rion to take full control over his body and his orgasm.

Nick bent his knees slightly and thrusted upward, but only gently to meet Rion's bottom when he slid downward. Rion began to moan, his eyes closed, and he rocked back and forth. He held onto Nick's shoulders and murmured, "So good, Nicky. It feels so good."

Nick found himself saying back, "You feel so good too, Ree... so, so good."

They moaned and murmured together until Rion said, "Gonna cum."

Nick reached between them and held onto Rion. It was all too much, the pressure on his inside and Nick's firm grasp on his outside organ. He cried out, and cum shot across Nick's chest in long ropes of four, five, six spurts before it lessened. Nick gave Rion a quick moment before he reached down and held onto Rion's cheeks. He began to pump upward, jerking and swaying Rion's body over him. He didn't mean to, but the intensity was so great he felt himself dig his nails into Rion's hips, and his lover cried out from above right before he came.

Rion rolled off Nick with a "holy, holy shit." He laid down on his back and sighed. Nick looked over at his sweaty, glowing body. His face was flushed red, and he had a satiated smile on his face.

"How does it feel?" he asked as he carefully rolled off the condom, tied it, and turned to his side.

Rion smiled. "It feels amazing. You're an amazing lover."

Nick found himself blushing. "Okay, thanks..." Rion chuckled and closed his eyes. He put one hand over his deflating organ and touched himself gently. Nick spoke again. "But what does it feel like... being...

when someone is ... inside of you? Not just me, just ... in general."

Rion smiled again. "Do you want me to tell you, or do you want me to show you?" he teased.

Nick didn't say anything for a long moment, thinking about their conversation earlier about consent while allowing Rion to come down from the high of his climax and return to normal. Rion was just about to speak when he heard Nick say, "I think I want you to show me."

Rion's eyes opened, then he narrowed them to slits and turned his head to look into Nick's eyes.

They stared at each other unblinkingly, and then Nick began to giggle. "Holy shit. I don't like the way you're looking at me right now, like a lion about to catch his prey."

Rion's mouth curved into a smile. "Oh, Nicky, you have no idea what you're asking, baby."

"I know what I'm asking, Ree," Nick said. "You told me to let you know. This is me letting you know."

Rion was thoughtful. "Okay. If you're serious, there are a couple of steps you need to take before I go there with you. To get you ready. And it's not going to be today. This is the first time you've said it, so I don't know how serious you are. Do these things, and I'll know you're serious."

Nick chucked. "Okay. Like what?"

"Step one, clean out."

Nick looked at him, confused. "Clean out? Clean out...?" Rion raised an eyebrow at him. "Oooh!" Nick's eyes widened with recognition, and he started laughing again. "So what, do I take a full enema?"

"No, you don't have to go that far. I'm not asking you to clean your entire colon," Rion said. "A bulb or a shower pump will do."

"A what?"

Rion explained the ins and outs of male douching. Nick was in awe. "So men really do this? *You* do this?"

Rion nodded. "At least once a week. Twice a week this month because of you."

"You're shitting me!" he said in surprise. "Pun intended."

"I shit you *not*. Pun intended," Rion said with a smirk.

Nick laughed. "I've never seen you do it the whole time we've been here."

"And why would I let you see me do it?" Rion asked back.

Nick opened his mouth, but no words came out at first. "Okay. Clean out. Got it. Next?"

"Stretch out."

Nick gave him a confused look. "You can't just stretch me out?" he said as he touched Rion's thigh.

"I could. But I don't think you want that," Rion said, moving closer and putting his hand on Nick's thigh, too. "Practice makes perfect."

"Okay. So what's the best way to stretch out?"

Rion explained different anal toys that could help. "Buy a couple, try them on your own. Figure out what you like and what you don't like."

Nick nodded. "And when I've done that? What's step three?"

Rion moved even closer. "Then you have to come find me," he said on Nick's lips. "You come to me. Tell me you want me to take you. Because consent is sexy to me. I won't touch you until you have completed all three steps."

Nick was again in awe. "Wow. You're an aggressive lover, aren't you?"

Rion leaned back and said, "I'm a very patient lover. Until I'm not." He narrowed his eyes and gave Nick a sultry look again.

Nick couldn't turn away from Rion's brown eyes even if he wanted to. "I've never been so afraid in my life," said Nick.

Rion moved closer, kissed Nick's lips, and put his head on Nick's chest. He ran his fingers down his stomach and reached down to hold onto his cock.

"You should be."

The next morning, Rion woke to Nick's head on his chest, his arms around his torso, surprised that he woke up first. It felt different this time than the last time they were heading to Heathrow. It was more final, but maybe Nick was onto something by coming back. Leaving Nick at the airport nearly broke him before, but he felt more prepared to leave Nick when they parted this time. He began to stroke Nick's hair, waking him up.

"Hmmm," Nick responded.

"We have lots to do today, baby," he said softly.

"Hmmm... let's stay here forever instead," Nick mumbled with his eyes closed.

"Okay," Rion agreed. "When you're ready."

After a moment, Nick rose and looked into his eyes. "I'll never be ready to leave you."

"Don't say things like that, Nicky," Rion said quietly.

Nick responded by lying back down on Rion's chest. They didn't talk for another twenty minutes until Nick said, "Let's take a shower and go out for breakfast."

"Okay," Rion agreed.

They went to eat a proper English breakfast at a nearby café. Rion made sure he paid for it. The pair sat quietly, eating and watching each other, trying to create a mental picture to keep in their memory. Afterward, they walked around holding hands, taking pictures of each other and selfies together, stopping in stores and buying gifts for their individual nieces and nephews, avoiding words about their impending separation. They made sure to grab snacks, a huge bag of Cool Ranch Doritos, skittles, and miniature Hershey's Kisses to share on the flight.

Eventually, they headed back to the hotel and packed their bags fully. Once done, Nick and Rion lay in bed fully clothed, talking less, staring more, and napping in between.

When Rion woke, Nick was already up, watching him. "Hey, babe. Gourmet burger for dinner?" he asked.

"Nope. I want the works," Rion said with a smile. "Lobster. Duck. Whatever sheep or lamb that was killed this morning, I want on my plate for my last supper."

Nick laughed. "Whatever you want, you got it."

They ate a lobster dinner at the hotel restaurant, then went to Hyde Park and walked around, holding hands one last time. At 7 p.m., they went back to the hotel room to grab their bags and headed downstairs to check out together.

"And how was your stay, Mr. Highton?" the receptionist asked.

"Life-changing," Nick said seriously, making Rion smile behind him.

"Well, I am glad we could make that happen for you," the receptionist said happily. "Please come again."

Nick turned around to see Rion's smiling face. He reached for his hand, and they left the hotel, getting the car service one final time to Heathrow Airport.

Their flight was leaving at 10:25 p.m., getting them to JFK around 2 a.m. Eastern Standard Time. Their seats, 17E and 17F, were on the other side of the plane from where they sat before, and the plane was much more full than the last time. As the safety announcements began, Nick saw nervousness all over Rion's face and asked, "Why do you sit near the window if you don't like being up in the air?"

"I like the view," Rion responded. "I just don't like the taking off and the landing. Once we're in the air, I'm fine."

"And now you have to do it twice, get off this plane and go to your connecting one."

"Ugh, don't remind me," Rion groaned.

Nick reached over and took his hand. "Want me to go with you?"

"Yes," Rion said honestly. "And move in with me and stay forever."

Nick smiled and leaned over to kiss his cheek. "Okay."

Rion shook his head. "You suck at clean breaks."

"I do," he admitted. "If you really want a clean break from me, you're going to have to initiate it."

"Maybe what I want now is a friendship? A long-distance one?" Rion asked tentatively.

"Yeah, we can do that," Nick agreed. "No pressure. Just checking in every once in a while, making sure the other is okay. As long as we're not in the same space, I can resist you."

Rion laughed. "That means no getting on planes and popping into San Francisco like you did in London."

Nick laughed back. "Deal. That means you can't just jump on a plane and come to New York either, without warning."

"Pffft! The chances of that happening are slim to none. I'm not getting on a plane again for the next couple of years." Comically, the plane began to move at that exact moment. "Shit," he murmured.

"I'm right here, baby," Nick murmured back. He held onto Rion's hands as the plane moved faster.

Rion shut his eyes tight and leaned back into the chair. He held onto Nick tightly until they were upright in the air, then slowly let go. He opened his eyes to see Nick looking at him. "What?"

"Nothing. Just memorizing the beautiful face in front of me," Nick said.

Rion's mouth turned upside down. He lifted the armrest between them and leaned onto Nick's shoulder.

They spoke softly, talked about Nick's magazine and the plans for it, talked about Rion's book and the plans for that. They watched a movie together, ate bad airline food, and played cards on Nick's computer. Rion fell asleep, as Nick expected. He woke up with his head in Nick's lap as Nick was reading his novel, gently touching his curls.

"Did you get to the good part yet?" Rion asked.

"You mean when he rode his best friend like Seabiscuit? Yeah, I got to that part," Nick said without taking his eyes off the book. Rion chuckled. "You were in a deep sleep for the last hour."

"It's funny because I don't sleep deeply. It's the other reason why I use CBD, it calms my anxiety, but it also helps me to sleep."

"You haven't used it all month. Unless you've been taking edibles behind my back."

Rion was thoughtful. "No. I haven't used it all month. I didn't need to. Being with you, the sex, the cuddling, the comfort, it all helped me sleep. And I wasn't anxious the whole time because you made me feel relaxed. I think you might be my new drug, Nick."

Nick smiled. "I know you're mine."

Rion smiled with his face still on Nick's thighs. They laid in silence until the announcement came on. "Ladies and gentlemen, we will be descending into JFK International Airport in thirty-five minutes. Please search around for your belongings and begin to shut down your electronics and fold your tray tables."

Rion sat up, feeling his chest begin to tighten, not sure whether it was because of the landing that was about to happen or the separation from Nick, also about to happen. He put on a brave face and gave Nick a smile, then began to clean up around them like they did the last time they were on a plane together. They packed up their belongings, lifted the trays to the back of the chairs in front of them, and adjusted their seats upright.

"Shit!" Rion said out loud as he felt the first movement of descent, and his ears began to clog.

"What?"

"I forgot gum. It's okay. I'll chew candy." He reached down for his book bag under the seat in front of him when Nick gently touched his arm.

"You just need to keep your mouth and jaw moving, right?"

"Yeah, that's the general idea."

Nick touched his chin and lifted it up to him. "So, let's keep your mouth moving." He kissed Rion's lips and slipped his tongue in between them.

Rion's hand cradled the side of Nick's neck. "I don't think this is going to work," he said in between returning his kisses.

"Only one way to find out," Nick said, and slid his tongue into Rion's mouth again.

They held onto each other and opened their mouths wider, mimicking the other's movements. Rion closed his eyes and moved his face to Nick's neck. He began to suck gently, then harder, not feeling the little bounces of turbulence as he held onto Nick's torso tightly. Nick ran his fingers around the nape of Rion's neck. When Rion had done enough damage, turning Nick's alabaster neck a mauve color, he lifted his face up, and Nick's lips immediately crash-landed upon him again. They kissed hungrily, greedily, never wanting to let go, until the bump of the wheel on the tarmac took them both out of their kiss, breaking the connection.

Rion gasped and pulled back, looking into Nick's eyes. Nick's face mirrored his awe. Then he smiled first. As people began to gather around them, Rion lifted the armrest, and Nick unbuckled his seatbelt and reached over to unbuckle Rion's. Rion put his arms around Nick's neck and pulled their bodies closer. There they sat with their eyes closed, not knowing or caring who saw them, until the majority of the passengers were already off the plane. Rion slowly released his arms and stood up.

Nick took that as his cue and stood up as well. He stepped into the aisle and pulled his carry-on down. Rion grabbed his book bag and slipped it on his back. He walked in front of Nick but reached back, and Nick took his hand. They came off the plane together, hand in hand, all the way to the walkway near the gate. There they faced each other.

Rion was speechless. Nick came closer and reached one arm around his shoulder, the other under his armpit. Rion did the same. They held each other tightly, then Nick whispered, "I love you, Rion Matthews."

Rion let a breath pass, then said, "I love you, too, Nicholas."

Nick leaned up and kissed his lips, then let go. He turned around and headed in the opposite direction of Rion without a glance back.

Rion watched him walk away until he disappeared in the crowd, then turned to the sign that said, "Connecting Flights," and followed the path to the next plane.

oey Huffnagle saw Nicholas slide away and immediately gravitated to him. "What do you need, Boss?"

Every event Nick had attended for the last four years, Zoey went to as well, just so he could keep her close. She didn't mind being one of the many unknown faces at the events the Hightons and other wealthy families put on annually. She was his friend, his bodyguard, his concierge, anything he needed her to be, and she enjoyed the thrill of being needed day or night. Zoey was the wife of a struggling playwright and was paid handsomely for being at Nick's beck and call, as she was that evening.

Nick needed something, anything, to put some distance between Penny's squawking and his mother's nagging. He was grateful to Zoey for her presence and for reading him so well. "I need you to find Penny a car to take her home later this evening," he said sternly.

"Home... Home to your apartment or..." She raised an eyebrow.

"No. To her apartment on the East side."

"Understood," she said with a nod. "And if she has questions?"

"I don't care, make something up," Nick said grouchily. "Just as long as she doesn't go home with me tonight."

"On it," she said automatically and walked away, already on her phone making arrangements.

Nick stepped onto the stone balcony of his parents' home and looked up at the moon. The fireworks would be starting soon, but he was not interested in fireworks. He was only interested in one thing. He picked up his phone and dialed the number with the 415 area code.

Rion answered right away. "Your ears must be ringing. I was looking up at the moon, thinking of you. Wondering if you were looking at the same moon, too."

"I was. Happy Fourth," Nick said to Rion.

"Happy Fourth, Nicky," Rion responded.

"What are you doing?" he asked. "Besides thinking of me."

"What all red-blooded Americans are doing today. Sitting in someone's backyard talking shit and eating ribs." Rion gave his friends a nod and got up from around the pool area. "And how are you celebrating America's birthday?" Rion asked as he found a quiet place in the yard and sat down. He switched the phone to his other ear and held onto his beer.

"How our family always does it, with the event of the season," Nick said dryly. "We have two, the Fourth of July one that is affectionately called 'A Midsummer Night's Dream,' and the Halloween party, which is called 'The Masquerade Gala.' Both are ostentatious and obnoxious."

"And I'm sure Madeline thanks you for being the dutiful son."

"Yup, I'm playing all the roles she needs me to play tonight," he said, bored.

Rion was quiet, then asked, "So, boyfriend, too?"

Nick hesitated, then said, "Uh-huh."

"Hmmm... So I guess tonight is your once-monthly sex duty?"

Nick sighed. "Rion... I'm not..."

But he trailed off because he didn't have anything to say. He wasn't going to sleep with Penny tonight, but he knew he would again at some point. "How's the WIP coming along?" Nick asked, wanting to change the subject.

"I haven't picked it up in four days."

"Since you've been back? Why?"

"I've just been feeling a little ... stuck."

"Well, run some ideas past me," Nick said happily, having something to do.

"I'm just struggling with why Darren is putting up with Will's family. Why does Will allow them to treat him like shit, and they don't even know that they're together yet? I'm trying to put myself in the space where something like that would happen. Because I personally would have walked away."

Nick got comfortable in the backyard chaise. "Well, it sounds like Darren understands Will's predicament, such as having to walk the line of pleasing his family, since it doesn't sound like he has ever stood up to them. But at the same time, Will needs Darren in his life. Trixie explained it as ignoring the pin in her shoe just so she could get to walk beside me. And as far as why Will allows them to treat him like shit... Maybe he doesn't, after a while. Maybe he's biding his time until he can grow some balls and make his great escape with Darren. Maybe Darren just needs to be a little more patient."

"Or maybe Darren should just walk away before his feelings for William end up tearing him apart," said Rion.

"Is that how you want your story to go?" Nick asked. Rion didn't answer. "Are we still talking about your story, Rion?"

"We've spoken every night like this is going to continue. Why?"

"Because it's hard to let go of this special connection we have. I'm not ready to let go. Are you?"

Rion was about to respond when they both heard a voice behind him. "Nicholas darling, the Benningtons are looking for us." Nick turned to see Penny standing there in her black beaded top, white pants, and straight blond hair. "Who are you talking to?"

"A friend," Nick responded. "I'll be inside shortly."

"Well, don't take too long, darling," she said and walked back inside the house.

Nick and Rion were both quiet. Nick began, "Rion—"

Rion cut him off. "So I'm going to be a little busy over the next couple of weeks. I really have to buckle down and get the manuscript together before the end of the year. I just wanted to give you a head's up."

"Okay," said Nick. "I know it's important to you."

"It is," Rion said right away. "I've been slacking since we got back, and I need to get my head back in the game. So if I'm unavailable, you know why. In fact, I think I'm gonna go. You've given me some things to think about, and I should get home and get to work."

"Well, don't disappear on me completely now," Nick teased. "Take breaks, and let me make you smile once in a while."

"I can't just take breaks, Nick. This is my career, you know," Rion said, almost annoyed. "Not all of us can choose to work or not to work and have a trust fund to fall back on."

"Ouch," Nick said. Rion didn't respond. "Okay. Just um... call me when you come up for air. Okay, Ree?"

"Yup."

"Ree?"

"Yeah, Nick?"

"You still mean a lot to me," Nick said. Rion didn't respond. "I just... I wanted you to know that."

"Yeah. I know. Me too." Rion replied distractedly. "I really have to go, Nick."

"Yeah, okay, sure." He paused. "I'll um... wait for you to call me."

"Yeah. I will. Soon. And thanks for your advice on Darren and William. Your perspective is important."

"You're a fantastic writer, Rion. This story will be fantastic because you're writing it."

Rion closed his eyes, his heart already aching for what he was about to do. "Thanks. Goodbye, Nicky."

"Bye, Ree. Happy Fourth."

"Yeah. Happy Fourth." Rion hung up first.

Nick continued to hold on to the phone as the fireworks began to light up the sky. He had a feeling in the pit of his stomach that he wouldn't be hearing from Rion for a while, if ever again.

Nick stepped off the elevator on his floor after his gym workout that Sunday morning and turned toward his door. Penny was standing there ringing the doorbell, looking perturbed.

"Penelope?" he called out.

She was startled at someone calling her name and touched her chest as she looked at him, then relaxed. "Oh, Nicholas. I was beginning to worry."

"What are you doing here?" he asked as he came closer and used his key to let them both in.

"Well, is that any way to treat your lady?" she said amusedly.

He did not answer. Instead, he held the door open for her to walk in, then closed it and went right into his kitchen for a glass of water. He stood on one side of the island as she made herself comfortable sitting on the stool on the other side.

They stared at each other until she said, "Well, hello, Nicholas."

"Hello, Penny," he said politely. "Mind telling me why you are at my door at 8 a.m. on a Sunday morning?"

"I was visiting my cousin in the city, stayed in my apartment last night, and decided to stop by this morning before heading back. Is it a crime for me to stop by?"

"You don't stop by, especially without notice. What if I wasn't here?"

"Then you wouldn't be here, and I would try again another day," she said factually. "But I'm glad you are. It's been a while since we've talked."

He sighed. "We were just together last month on the Fourth," he reminded her.

"But we didn't talk because you left the party early and sent me to my apartment in the city instead of yours. And we haven't seen each other this whole month."

"So you're here because we haven't had sex in three months?" Nick asked seriously.

She made a sour face. "Must you be so crass? I'm here because we haven't talked. I feel like we haven't really talked since your trip to London in June. You came home and then turned around so quickly and went right back. I didn't even know you had left until your assistant, Zelda, told me you had an emergency and needed to return to London. I didn't even know when you got back."

"Zoey," Nick said as he kept his face neutral and continued to sip his water. "Her name is Zoey."

"Yeah, whatever, the fat lady," Penny said dismissively. Nick narrowed his eyes at her as she kept talking. "I just think it's not kind or polite to disappear on me like that. We're supposed to be a team, Nicholas. I should know where you are at all times, and you should know where I am at all times, without the use of personal assistants. How else is this partnership going to work?" Nick remained quiet. "You don't have anything to say for yourself, Nicholas?"

"I'm sorry if I made you worry," he said flatly.

Penny blinked at him a few times, then conceded with a sigh. "What am I going to do with you, Nick?"

He didn't answer. Instead, Nick exited his kitchen on the other side of the island and said, "I'm going to go take a shower." He didn't wait for a response; he walked to his bedroom and closed his door.

Nick jumped into the shower and closed his eyes. He thought of Rion's face, how his curly hair got matted against his forehead when wet, how his dark eyelashes and curly chest hair dripped water droplets, how curved his pecs were, how frosted pink his nipples were. Nick absentmindedly stroked his cock, thinking about Rion's wide mouth down his shaft. He continued stroking to bring himself to ejaculation when there was a knock on the bathroom door.

"You can't stay in there all day, Nicholas. We need to talk." Penny's voice came through the closed door.

"Fuck me," he breathed out softly.

With his cock already softening at the sound of her voice, Nick turned the water to lukewarm and properly washed and dried himself off. He came out of the bathroom in his robe, and Penny was sitting on the bed with her legs crossed. She looked up at him and then stood up and began to unbutton her blouse.

"Don't," Nick said sharply. Penny paused, then resumed getting undressed. "You said we needed to talk. You didn't say we needed to fuck."

"Must you be so vulgar?" she asked as she slipped off her shirt and unhooked her bra.

Penny's D cups came flopping against her chest. To the average man, they were perfect, round and large, what dreams were made of. Penelope paid handsomely for them almost three years ago, along with her tummy tuck and nose job. But Nick always found them to be too large and too much in the way. He preferred smaller breasts that he could hold in his hand; the smaller the better. Or no breasts at all.

Once her pencil skirt was off, along with her matching slip and underwear, she walked closer to him and put her hands on his shoulders. She kissed his lips and made her way down to her knees, still in her black pumps, untying his robe. One thing that Nick was never able to resist was a blow job, even an average one, so he let it happen. Penny took Nick in her mouth and went halfway down and back up. Nick couldn't help but compare. Her suction was nowhere near Rion's, her mouth not tight enough and deep enough. But Nick hadn't had sex with another person since he left London, so her mediocre mouth was enough to make him rise.

*Fuck it*, he said to himself.

He grabbed her by her arm roughly and pulled her to her feet, startling her. "What are you—"

"Shut up, Penny," he said, almost angrily. "You want to be fucked? Let's fuck."

"Nick!" she exclaimed. But she allowed him to push her onto the bed face down, her feet still on the floor.

He reached between her legs and found her semi-wet, not nearly enough, so he licked his fingers and played with her. She began to moan, and it sounded so fake to him. But he didn't care. He kept going, touching her until she was wet enough. He stood up and slid inside of her easily and began to pump. Nick closed his eyes and pretended it was Rion's hole he was pounding into. He had to bite his lip a few times not to call out Rion's name. Penny hollered and climaxed right before Nick's mind went blank, and he released inside of her. The moment he came, he felt guilty, like he had cheated on someone that wasn't even around, someone that wasn't his.

Nick stood up, grabbed his robe off the floor, and wiped his penis with it. Penny stood up and finger-combed her hair. She gave Nick an apathetic look, then went into the bathroom and closed the door. Soon he heard the shower going. He hated that she did that, showered almost immediately after sex with him. It made him feel dirty. He missed Rion, how they would cum all over their bodies and then hold each other afterward, laying in their mess until one of them had to take a piss. He thought about Rion's view of sexy consent, and it made him ashamed of how he had treated Penny just then. He vowed to be nicer to her for the rest of the day, for Rion's sake.

Nick took his phone off the dresser and opened it with his fingerprint. He looked through his pictures and found the one of Rion in Hyde Park, lying in the sun, eyes closed, fingers laced on his stomach, a look of contentment on his face. He missed Rion so much that his heart ached. He thought of texting him, but he knew it would not go anywhere. Rion had not responded to Nick's texts since the Fourth of July, and Labor Day would be in a week. He put his phone down and began to get dressed. He went into the kitchen and started making himself a breakfast shake, turning on the TV to CNN because he knew she hated it.

Penny came out of the room thirty minutes later, fully dressed, and her makeup retouched. She sat next to him on the couch, and he ignored her, quietly sipping his shake and watching the state of affairs as told by Victor Blackwell.

"We need to talk," she spoke first. He continued to ignore her, so she reached over and took the remote to turn off the TV. "Nicholas? Did you hear me?"

"I heard you," he said calmly, staring at the blank screen.

"Well?"

"Well, what?"

Penny gave him a look of frustration and fin-ger-combed her blond hair again. "Nicholas, I think it's time we talked about our future."

Nick paused mid-sip, and his eyes wandered over to her. She was sitting with her ankles crossed and her hands connected in her lap like a schoolteacher giving a lecture. Nick was not in the mood for a lecture.

"What future, Penelope?"

"We've been together for over two years, Nicholas. Don't you think it's time?"

"Time for what?" he asked with an eyebrow raised.

"To begin talking about marriage and children. Where we're going to live, here in the city or in Buffalo. A future, Nicholas. Don't you want that?"

"What on God's green earth gave you the impres-sion that I wanted that?" Nick said, bewildered.

Penny looked shocked, then confused, then annoyed. "I don't understand. Are you saying you never want to get married? Do you plan on being a bachelor forever?"

Nick thought about it. He actually did want to get married at some point, maybe start a family, but having children was not that important to him. And it was not going to be with the woman sitting before him. Rion's face popped into his head again. He remem-bered his conversation with him about Penny. He had to let her go.

He turned his body to her. "Penelope, I think we need to be honest with ourselves and each other. We are not compatible. We don't love each other. We are not on the same page. I think it's time to let this go."

She blinked at him a few times. "What are you talking about, Nicholas?" Penny asked calmly. "It's already been established. It's just a matter of us setting a date and coming out with it."

It was Nick's turn to blink at her a few times before he asked calmly, "Established by who?"

"Our parents, silly," she said automatically. "They have already approved this union. It's time to make it official."

Nick looked away from her as fear gathered in his chest. He stood up and walked over to the kitchen. "Penny—"

"Nick, I know it's a lot to take in, but it will be fine," she said, as if they were deciding where to eat for dinner. "I can handle all the arrangements. I just wanted you to know that I'm starting to put things in motion for us. But we have to do better at communicating our wants and needs. For example, I need you to tell me if you're going out of town, so I don't look like a fool when people ask me where my husband is. Do you think you can do that?"

Nick didn't answer. He was staring at his reflection on his toaster, watching the color drain from his face as someone else made his life decisions for the next fifty years. Penny came over to him and touched his shoulders.

"Nicholas, relax. It will be—"

"Penelope," he said sharply as he turned around. "I can't do this. I can't marry you. I'm sorry."

She looked confused. "What are you saying, Nick?"

He stared at her like she had two heads. "I said," Nick began, speaking very slowly, "That I ... am not ... marrying ... you."

"You mean like next year or..."

"What the fuck!" Nick found himself yelling, startling the both of them. He walked away from her to stand in front of the picture window in the living room. "You should go."

"Okay," she said, too calm for his liking. "I can see this is not the right time to have this conversation. You seem to be very stressed. We'll talk about when to announce our engagement—"

"Fuck, Penelope, you're not listening to me!" Nick yelled again, whirling around to face her. "We need to break up. Now. Right now. I don't want ... this ... *thing*... this arrangement we have anymore. I'm done pretending for our families that we're happy. I'm not happy with you. And you know you're not happy with me. So it's over. We're done. You should go. And never return to my apartment again."

Penny sighed and placed one hand on the island. "Is this because of Beatrice?"

Nick's mouth dropped before he could stop himself, but he closed it back up and gave her a hard look. "Oh, I'm sorry. I mean *Trixie*," she said with disdain. "Are you still in love with the farm girl Trixie after all this time?"

"What do you know about Trixie?" He returned his face to its neutral state.

She sighed and rolled her eyes at the same time. "Everything, Nicholas. I know everything about her. I know you loved her, and your family forced you two apart. I know that she took the money that your parents gave her because her farm and her family were more important to her than you. I know that she is married to a boy from her high school, has two children, and runs the produce market now. All that brains she received at Harvard to have her still milking cows and shucking corn is beyond me." She shrugged.

"Three."

"Excuse me?"

"She has three children now," Nick confirmed. "She just had a son this year, Logan, named after her favorite X-Men character. You're not the only one that knows things."

"Well, then, you know she is happy and doesn't think about you at all," Penny said factually. "It's fine if you're still in love with her. I'm not threatened by that. But you will love her from afar and commit to this partnership."

Nick realized at that moment that he hated Penny. He asked Rion for forgiveness in his head for how mean he was about to get with her. "I'm not in love with Trixie anymore. I'm in love with someone else."

Penny did not flinch. "Okay, fine. Just as long as you keep it private and away from our affairs. You can keep whatever sweetheart you have, like you've been doing with all the other women you've been sleeping with for the last two years. Just know I will not tolerate you embarrassing me, Nicholas. You will lose everything in a divorce if you do that. The prenup will ensure that."

"Do you hear yourself, Penny? I told you that I'm not going to marry you. I told you I'm in love with someone else. Do you understand that I don't want to be with you? How in the fuck are you talking about prenups and divorces—"

"Can you stop using such foul language, Nicholas?" she said as she touched her temples. "Must you be so vulgar?"

Nick had had enough. "Get the fuck out of my house."

She looked affronted. "Nicholas—"

He said it louder, "Get the FUCK out of my house!"

"Okay, fine. It's too much right now, I can tell." She grabbed her bag off the island and walked to the front door. "I'll call you later this week."

Nick went past her and opened the door. "Don't call me later this week. Don't call me again. This is over. And don't bother running to my mother crying about this like the last time. I'm not going to change my mind."

Penny went cold. "I did not run to your mother, Nicholas. The day after you broke up with me, she saw me at the golf club and asked me what was wrong, so I told her. And the next thing I knew, you were at my apartment in Buffalo. You came back to me, remember?"

"And that was a mistake," he said with his chin raised. "One I will not make a second time. You will make someone very happy one day. Just not me." He opened the door wider. "Goodbye, Penny."

She blinked at him a few times, then held her head up high and walked out of the apartment.

Nick closed the door behind her and leaned against it. He realized how quickly his heart was beating. He needed to talk to someone and thought about Rion but then remembered again, like he did many times a day, that Rion would not get his messages. He closed his eyes in anger, then sadness, before he went back to his living room couch and sat on it. He picked back up his shake and watched the blank screen, thinking about the fallout from breaking up with Penny, but also ready for it.

Nick walked back into his office after being on the floor all morning. He was printing documents off his computer to show the digital management team when he saw he had an email. He took a quick look at the name; it was Rion.D.Writer@gmail. His heart skipped a beat, and he immediately sat down. He stared at the first few words that Outlook showed without opening it: "Hey, it's me, Rion. I know you're pissed, but he..."

Nick didn't want to read it, but he wanted to read it so badly. Since Rion had either changed his number or blocked Nick's, he had no way of getting in contact with him. Rion must have taken his work email off his card and used it to communicate. Nick's shock turned into anger. It had been three months since they last spoke. *Why couldn't he just pick up the god-damn phone and talk to me?* he thought angrily.

Nick clicked on the email and opened it fully. He took his time reading it.

> Hey, it's me, Rion. I know you're pissed, but hear me out before you delete this message. I know I said we should still be friends, but you and I both know how hard that would be, for both of us. We kept agreeing that we needed a clean break from each other, but we had never actually done it. And you said I had to be the one

to initiate because you never would have. I had to do it for both of us. Especially since I needed to focus on meeting my deadline for this new story, which is coming out great, by the way. I've already sent the first 100 pages to my editor, and he loves it. I can't wait for you to read it, Nicky. If you think Jet Lagged was full of twists and turns, you just wait.

Anyway, I wanted you to know that I'm okay. And I hope you are, too. And I have a favor to ask. I took a picture of you when you were sleeping, remember? I ran my hands through your hair and took a picture of our hands touching. My editor wants to use it for the cover. It doesn't show your face, just the top of your head and our hands. That's the name of the story, by the way, Connecting Hands. You'll see when you read it. So anyway, I just wanted to officially ask you if it is okay that I use your image. I can compensate you for it if that helps. Just let me know what you need.

So yeah. I miss you, Nicky. A lot. I know I'm not acting like it, but RWAWN2. That won't ever change for me.

Love, Ree

At the bottom of the email was a black-and-white photo. Nick could see it was him, but no one else would be able to tell. His arm was over his face, touching his hair and Rion's hand was in his hair, connecting their fingers. It was sensual and romantic. Nick remembered the morning when he had woken to Rion running his hands through his hair, his professional camera on the bed between them. Nick's heart and cock began to ache.

Marcel knocked on his open door, pulling him out of his memory. "Your meeting with the digital team is starting without you, Boss."

"Thanks, Marcel," he said unemotionally.

Marcel gave his supervisor a confused look and came over. "You okay, Boss? You look sad."

Nick shook it off. "I'm good. Tell Nguyen and Archer I'll be over in a moment. Thanks," he said dismissively, and Marcel knew that was his cue to go away.

Nick replied to the email:

Yes, you can use my image for your novel. Good luck. Nick.

He closed out his email and met his staff for the next meeting.

"Nicholas. Darling," she started.

"Good morning, Mother," he responded.

Madeline called her son every Friday morning. He assumed it was out of habit and not genuine care, and the first Friday in October was no different. Or so he thought.

"I just got your and Penny's RSVP for the Masquerade Gala on October 31st. I'm so pleased that you will be attending with her."

"You mean your Halloween party?" Nick said amusedly. Then he realized what she had said. "Mother, I'm not going with Penny. I told you it's over between us. I haven't spoken to her in a month."

"Yes, yes, that's what you said," his mother said dismissively. "She understands that you're going through a hard time and will be there to support you when you're ready to come back to her."

Nick rolled his eyes. "I don't know if cotton is stuck in you and her ears every time I talk, but you both need to hear me and hear me good. Penny and I are not getting back together."

"Oh, Nicholas, why must you be so difficult about these things? If not Penny, then who?" Nick didn't answer. "You're twenty-seven years old, and Penelope is your best prospect at a full life with marriage and children. By thirty, you should be married with at least one child."

"Mother, not this again," he groaned.

"Nicholas, the purpose of life is to contribute to this earth meaningfully. If your work is not contributing meaningfully, and your lifestyle and the company you keep is questionable at best, the least you can do is have an acceptable wife by your side."

Nicholas ignored the dig at his career choices and friendships. "I don't love her, Mother. I'm not going to be in a loveless marriage."

"Of course you love her, dear, just not in a romantic way," said Madeline dismissively again. "And if you don't feel like you love her, it's because you haven't allowed yourself to. I've watched you fight your feelings for Penelope for years. You two belong together. You'll see. Just give it time."

"Mother—"

"Just accompany her to the gala, Nicholas. That's all I'm asking you to do. Stand by her side and be there for her. Do you care about her enough to do that?"

He sighed. "Sure. I can do that for her."

"Wonderful," she said gleefully. "I'll send a car around 8 p.m. for you and her at your home. Thank you, my son."

Nick rolled his eyes again. "You're welcome, Mother."

11

*R*ion was deep into a sex scene when someone knocked on the door. "Who is it?" he called out from his desk by the window, still typing. The apartment was small enough.

"Jay."

Rion stopped typing abruptly and did a small intake of breath. He had been avoiding everyone's calls, especially Jason's. He needed to finish his manuscript by the beginning of December and had less than two months to do it. He realized he had not answered until Jason called out again.

"Rion? Rion, open the door."

Rion didn't want to, but then again, he did. He had not laid eyes on Jason since before he had left for London. He didn't even know how Jason knew he was back. He slowly got up and realized firstly that he was in boxer briefs and nothing else, and secondly, was sprouting a hard-on; that was how engrossed he was in creating Darren and William's first sex scene in their senior year of college.

"One sec," he called out as he quickly ran to the room and grabbed a pair of sweats to put on.

Once done, he opened the door. There Jason stood in all of his caramel-skinned glory, diamond studs in both ears, light brown eyes, and thick lips. He smiled at Rion, and Rion found himself smiling back but then quickly turned around. Jason let himself in and went to the fridge first.

"You have beer?"

"Nothing but White Claw in there. Gotta get to the store."

Rion made his way back to his desk and reread his descriptions of his characters' lovemaking. He looked at Jason bent over in his fridge, how tight his ass looked in his dark blue jeans, and felt his cock tighten in his sweatpants. *Shit*, he thought. He closed his laptop.

Jason stood back up with a raspberry-flavored drink and popped open the can. He smiled at Rion as he sat on the couch and purposely opened his legs as wide as they would go, looking down at Rion's hairy chest and nipples before his eyes found his face.

"You didn't tell me you were back."

Rion shrugged. "I didn't know I needed to announce it to you."

Jason nodded slowly. "So, how was it? Did you get what you needed for your book?"

Rion's mind immediately went to Nick. Nick thrusting into him as he lay on his back. And on his stomach. And his side. Riding Nick's cock on the terrace. And on the couch. And on the hallway floor. His cock swelled again.

"Yeah. I got what I needed. And then some," he answered.

Jason nodded again. "Well, come here. I don't bite. Unless you ask."

"I don't think that's a good idea, Jay."

"Because we're on a break?" he asked.

Rion rolled his eyes. "We're not on a break. We're done. We've been done for months."

"You didn't say that in May when you were riding my dick over the same desk you're sitting at."

Rion's words caught in his throat. But then he said, "That was a mistake. And I told you that."

"Rion, c'mon," he said. "You know you can't stay away from me, and I can't stay away from you. You belong with me."

Nick's face came into his mind again. "No, I don't belong to you, and you don't belong to me. You need a partner that's going to be all in with you. I'm not that guy anymore."

Jason stared at him. "Can't you just be the guy that's all in right now?"

Rion sighed. "Is that why you came over here?"

"Yes. And no," Jason said with a smirk. He stood up and came closer to Rion, who was still sitting in his desk chair. "I came over because Ava stopped by the bank this morning and mentioned that you were back. That you've been back since July. I wanted to see you, to make sure you were okay. That's the most important thing." He touched Rion's shoulders. "You know that all I ever want to do is take care of you."

Rion looked him in the eyes. "I don't need you to take care of me. I can take care of myself. We've had this argument before."

"And I'm not here to argue," Jason said right away. "I just wanted you to know that I'm thinking of you. That I miss being with you."

He touched Rion's neck and bent down to kiss his lips. Rion did not resist, although he immediately felt like he was cheating on Nick. Nick, who he had not spoken to in three full months, since he had blocked his number, and it felt like a lifetime ago. Nick, who had a girlfriend and lived three thousand miles away and was completely unavailable. Nick, who he had to let go of because Nick never would let go. Rion let his ex-lover kiss him, put his tongue in his mouth, ran his hand down to his nipple, and touched his hard-on. Jason moaned when he discovered Rion's secret, thinking that the hard-on was because of his arrival.

Suddenly, Rion could not remember why he was resisting Jason's affection. He hadn't had sex in months. *It's not like he was ever going to see Nick again, right?* he thought.

Rion stood up quickly. "You're clean?"

"Always," Jason said.

"Get on the couch. Face down," Rion demanded.

Jason grinned and followed his instructions. Rion went into his room and came out with a tube of Astroglide. Jason had already taken off his shoes and pants, leaving his white socks on, lying flat on Rion's green couch. Rion lubed up Jason, then only pulled his sweats and underwear down to the bottom of his thighs. He entered Jason carefully, unprotected, as was their unspoken agreement. They wore condoms with everyone else but only barebacked with each other.

Once Rion bottomed out, he began a slow thrust into Jason, and Jason moaned. Rion held onto the edge of the couch and closed his eyes. He couldn't help it. He imagined it was Nick he was thrusting into; Nick, who was an anal virgin but spoke about Rion being his first. He wondered if Nick would ever come to him for it. His brain went back to the first time Nick was inside of him, right on the glass coffee table. Rion moaned loudly and moved faster. He didn't know, realize, or care when Jason came; Rion was fucking someone else the whole time.

He thought about the feel of Nick's cock in his anus, in his mouth, Nick's tongue in his ass, deep throating his shaft, then looking up at him with his bright blue eyes.

"Oh God... Oh God," he heard himself moaning like the first time.

He started pounding harder, imagining how Nick would moan with his cock deep inside of him. It drove him over the edge faster than anything else could have. His body seized up, and he moved slower as he felt his cock dump a ton of semen inside Jason's tight brown bottom.

As the last spurts released, Rion called out his name in a whisper, "Nicky." Then he gasped, and his eyes flew open.

Rion froze, praying that Jason hadn't heard him, but it was nearly impossible since his face was so close to his head. His worst fear was confirmed when Jason said with an attitude from below him, "Who ... The FUCK ... Is Nicky?"

*Shit*, Rion thought for the second time.

He slowly pulled out of Jason and sat on the couch. Jason quickly stood up, Rion's cum trailing down his leg. Normally, Rion would have thought it was sexy, but the angry look on Jason's face made him think twice about mentioning it.

Jason asked nastily, "Who are you fucking, Rion?"

Rion did not back down. "Who are you fucking, Jason?"

"Fuck you. I'm not fucking anyone else."

"You're a fucking liar, and we both know it. You're fucking Shereen again."

"Everybody is fucking Shereen," Jason said, looking for his underwear. "Ever since she transitioned, she's going for the gold in cum deposits."

"I'm not fucking Shereen."

"Well, you're missing out, because she has a big dick," Jason said, sliding on his jeans. "And don't change the fucking subject. Who's Nicky?"

"Doesn't matter," Rion said and turned away.

"Oh, it matters if you're thinking about him when you're fucking me!" Jason said angrily.

"It doesn't matter because we're not together!" Rion yelled.

"Who? You and him or you and me!?"

"BOTH!" Rion screamed.

Rion stood up angrily and went to the kitchen on the other side of the open room. He pulled up his pants and sat on the counter, trying to figure out where it had all gone wrong. He watched Jason angrily put on his shoes, but then sit quietly on the couch, stewing in his own anger.

"I can't do this anymore," Rion said softly. "Sex with you is too confusing. It's not what I really want. It's just what's convenient and comfortable. You deserve better than that."

"Do you love him? Nicky?" Jason asked back just as softly.

"Yes," Rion admitted.

"Do you still love me?" he asked.

"I'm trying not to anymore because loving you is selfish; it's sending you mixed messages. But it gets easier when we're not ... fucking."

"You really don't want to be with me anymore?" Jason asked, his voice cracking.

It broke Rion's heart, but he had to let him go. "I really don't," he said. "And you shouldn't want to be with me. All I do is hurt you. You should want someone that wants to love you, that wants you to take care of them. That's not me, Jay."

Jason sat on the couch for a few moments more in silence. Then he stood up and made his way to the door without looking in Rion's direction. Rion jumped off the counter and ran to him, meeting him at the door.

"I'm sorry."

Jason nodded without looking at him. He reached for the knob, but Rion took his hand and held it. They looked at each other, then Jason put his forehead onto Rion's shoulder. He let a couple of tears drop, and Rion held him.

After a long moment, Jason leaned up. He wiped his face and gave Rion a chaste kiss on the lips. "Bye, Rion," said Jason.

He walked out the door before Rion could speak, so Rion said softly to himself, "Bye, Jay."

Penny showed up at Nick's apartment wearing a white gown with wings and a white and silver eye mask. She gasped at Nick's outfit. "You can't be serious," were the first words out of her mouth.

"What's wrong with my outfit? I'm Dracula."

"Didn't Zarina give you my specific instructions? You were supposed to be my guardian angel."

Nick ignored her purposely giving Zoey the wrong name. "I'd rather be the king of blood."

She scoffed. "I can't walk in with you if I'm wearing this and you look like ... *that*."

Nick smiled. "Then don't walk in with me," he said seriously. Penny scowled at him. His phone buzzed at the right time. He looked at it and said, "Come on, the car is downstairs."

They entered The Terrace Room at the Plaza Hotel together. Their picture was immediately taken, and they entered the stylish room, greeted by family, friends, and business partners. Penny dragged him around for the first hour until he was finally able to slink away when his brother's wife, Idalia, began a conversation with her. He moved closer to Brian.

"You okay, Nicholas?" Nick's brother asked quietly.

"Yeah, it's fine. It's the last event of the season that we'll be at together. I'll make sure of that," he said back quietly.

"Well, good luck with that," said Brian. "You know how Mother is."

Nick gave him a wry look and turned around. He left the ballroom and went to find a bathroom, bumping into a petite woman with curly brown hair. She was in a black leather dress with a metal brassiere.

"Oooh!" she called out, her bag dropping out of her hand, scattering items around.

"Sorry!" he said right away. They both bent down to pick up her items and bumped foreheads.

"Ow!"

"Oop! Sorry again!"

She fell backward and sat on the floor in laughter, her skirt hiking up. "I think I'll let you do the work." She took off her mask and put it on her head.

Nick bent over to pick up her items and glanced up, looking right into her thong, and immediately turned his head. He put things back into her purse and held his hand out to help her up, which she took.

"Thank you," she said.

He got a better look at her face, and his eyes went wide. "Hey, you're Kierra, the singer."

"Yes, I am," she said happily. "And you are...?"

"Nicholas Highton."

"Highton? So this is your fancy soiree?" she asked with a smile.

"My mother's," he said with a laugh. "I'm not this fancy."

"Oh, okay. She hired me to sing a couple of songs later and auction off this dress."

"That's aaah... some dress," Nick said, looking her up and down.

"Well, I'm glad you approve," Kierra said. She looked down and moved to pick up a miniature tube.

"I'll get that for you," he said as he went over to it.

"No, you don't have to— Shit," she said as he picked up the small bottle with the white powdery substance inside. He casually handed it to her and kept his face neutral. "Thanks," she said sheepishly.

"No problem," he said. "Can't wait to see your performance later."

She smiled. "I'll be looking for your face, Mr. Highton." She winked at him and went toward the ladies' room.

He watched her walk, thinking that she was his type: petite, small-breasted, with wide hips. He also noticed that her hair was the same shade and texture as Rion's. He sighed and went to the bathroom.

Nick was talking with one of his father's employees when Madeline Highton went onto the stage. "Before we hear from our entertainment tonight, I just want to acknowledge a few things. First..."

She began by thanking the committee for their hard work and made a special thank you to Penelope Benson's organization, Saving Grayce, which raised money for different causes and named the high-contributing donors one by one. Then she thanked her husband and her children for supporting her efforts over the years. Nick was barely paying attention until she started calling them and their spouses to the stage, his name last. He casually made his way to stand next to Brian, who was dressed like a surgeon in his typical work uniform. Nick pulled his mask to the top of his face, giving everyone a warm smile.

"Penny, can you join us, please," he heard his mother say.

Nick turned slowly to give his mother a look, but she would not glance in his direction, only smiling widely at Penny who indeed looked like an angel. She came over and stood next to him, then gently took his hand. Nick slowly turned to Penny, but she, too, would not look into his eyes.

"Penny has been such a wonderful addition to this family for many years. I have watched her grow into the beautiful, selfless, amazing young woman that she is. This is why it brings me nothing but great joy to announce the engagement of Penelope Benson to my son, Nicholas Highton. May their love and union last forever."

The applause was deafening as ice ran through Nick's veins. He looked out at the five hundred guests, happy for the union that he never sanctioned, and had the strongest urge to run, but his feet were frozen in place. He turned to look at Penny first; she smiled widely for him. She leaned over and kissed his cheek, squeezing his hand and waving to the crowd. He did not smile back. He turned all the way to the other side and looked at his mother, who was also smiling at him, but her eyes were cold. They said, "Don't you dare embarrass this family."

Nicholas realized two things at that moment: One, his mother was wrong. Smart girls were more important than pretty girls. Smart girls knew how to play the game and get what they wanted. And Penny was a very smart girl. His mother was a fucking genius.

Two, he hated both of these two manipulating women with a passion that was starting in the center of his chest and growing by the second. He didn't know whose idea it was, and it didn't matter. Both were going to pay dearly for this. They, and whoever else, that was part of the charade.

Nicholas looked at his brother, whose eyes went wide with a bewildered look. *What the fuck*, his brother mouthed to him. He knew that Brian did not know. He looked farther down at Emma's face. She was also not smiling. She caught his eye and immediately shook her head. *Good, so both of my siblings did not betray me*, he thought. For that, he was thankful. He searched the crowd for his father's face, but Niles was nowhere to be found. He had probably already figured it was going to be a bad outcome and didn't want anything to do with it.

Madeline came over and hugged them both quickly, then said into the microphone. "More information to come, but for now, please welcome Kierra!"

She gestured for them to walk off the stage single-file, and he did so, yanking his hand from Penny's grasp and almost knocking Kierra over as she came up the stairs. As soon as they hit the floor, the crowd surrounded them, telling him "congrats" and patting on his back. He was annoyed but quickly grateful for it because it put some distance between him and his fake fiancée. So he put on a smile and shook hands along the way.

Zoey, dressed as a nun, showed up out of nowhere and grabbed his arm. "Come with me," she said forcefully.

She pulled him toward the back of the room and rounded him with her confused eyes. "It's a lie," said Nick.

"Obviously," she said factually.

"Help me get out of it, Zoey," he pleaded.

"I can't, Boss. There is nothing you can do right now except smile and nod. But I am sending her home in a separate vehicle. Mostly to make sure you don't murder her tonight. We'll plan a public statement in about a month to announce your breakup, the same way they blindsided you with this engagement."

Zoey stood in front of him like a shield and shooed people away, saying, "Mr. Highton has a business matter to attend to. He'll find you afterward, thank you," giving him some time to think.

He leaned against the wall, trying to catch his breath as Kierra began to sing, and people forgot about him for a moment. When he felt well enough, he went toward the other side of the ballroom, as far away from Penny as the room would allow. Pissed was not even the word to describe how he felt. Of all the things his mother could have done to him, even pulling Trixie away, this underhanded way of putting him and Penny back together and making it public was unforgivable. They were going to learn once and for all not to fuck with him, his life, his future, or his freedom.

Nick started paying attention to the beautiful Kierra in her femme fatale outfit, singing her hit song, *Come Find Me*, and realized she was indeed looking at him, singing to him.

"If you want me/come find me/I can make it better babe/come find me/I can make it hotter babe/come find me/do you like no other babe/come find me..."

He picked up his phone and called Zoey, who was still in the ballroom. "Yes, Nick? What do you need? A getaway car?"

"Are there paparazzi in the crowd?" he asked, not taking his eyes off the singer.

"I think so. They follow Kierra everywhere."

"Find one. Tell them you'll have something for them in about an hour, in the sunroom right outside the downstairs bathrooms. But whatever they get, they have to wait three days before leaking the photos."

"Um ... okay. What are you planning, Boss?"

"One hour," he said without answering her question, then hung up.

Kierra continued to sing to him and only him. Nick gave her an obvious nod, and she smiled.

Kierra stepped up to the bar next to Nick. "Long Island Sunrise, please," she told the bartender.

Nick sipped his third cognac and said, "I'm supposed to come find you."

She laughed a sweet, girlish laugh and said, "Well, you looked like someone who got his head bashed in earlier, so I thought I should offer up my services first."

He turned to her. "What are you offering?"

"What do you want?" she asked seriously.

He leaned in and said in her ear, "Meet me in the downstairs sunroom. Bring your purse." He trailed his finger down the side of her arm before walking away.

Nick had taken off his mask and long coat and sat on the table looking up at the moon, biting his lip, lost in thought. He wondered what Rion was doing at that moment since it was already 8 p.m. there, and the sun had gone down on the west coast. He heard the door open but didn't turn around.

Kierra came to stand in front of him. "I take it you don't want to get married?"

"I don't want to get married to her," he said plainly.

"Then why did you propose?" she asked curiously.

"I didn't," he said sharply. "Apparently, my mother proposed on my behalf, and she accepted."

Her mouth dropped. "Oh, wow. Yeah, you need this."

She opened up her purse and pulled out the tube. She held out her left arm, then began to carefully put a line of coke across it. She lifted it up to him.

Nick had done coke a few times, but it wasn't his thing. He didn't like how it made him feel, except in moments like this when he didn't want to feel anything, to not give a fuck. But he needed to know one more thing before he went down this path. He ran his hands through her curly brown hair and thought of Rion again before he asked, "How old are you, Kierra? For real."

"My real name is Leslie, and I'm 23. But to the world, I'm 19."

He couldn't help but chuckle. She lifted up her arm to him again. He bent over, keeping eye contact with her, held one nostril closed, and sniffed. The feeling of euphoria immediately went to his brain. It made him feel bold, brave, and sexy. That he could conquer the world, master his own fate, and screw his mother and Penny over at the same time.

He watched Kierra make another line on her arm and take a hit. She rubbed her nose with her other hand and looked at him seductively. Nick took her arm and licked the remnants of the powder, then pulled her closer.

"**U**ncle Ree!" Morgan squealed when he came into Muriel's house.

She was always the first one to run into his arms, more so than his other niece and nephews. He picked her up and spun her around.

Ava greeted him on her way out. "Hey, baby bro, I'll be back."

"Where you going?" he asked. She had a face full of heavy makeup, a short, pleated skirt, and a bustier, her black hair with pink at the roots in two ponytails.

"Gonna go see a man about a horse," she called out. That was her way of saying for him to mind his business.

He shook his head and went to the living room and gave his youngest nephew, Jeff, a dap, gave his niece Katelyn a hug, and asked her about middle school, and didn't see his oldest nephew, Reese, but knew he would come in from playing with his friends right before Thanksgiving dinner.

Rion went into the kitchen to see his mother and sisters cooking. "Hey baby," his mother said first and came over to kiss his cheek.

"Hi, Roslyn," he said politely and moved over to his sister Muriel with a smile. He kissed her cheek and tried to take a meatball, only to get his hand slapped away by her. Even though she was half black, he looked the most like her, with the same color, curly brown hair, a thin nose, and full lips. They were also both the tall ones in their family, as Muriel was 5'11" and could have been a model if, in Rion's mind, she hadn't had such a shitty upbringing.

"How's the story coming along?" Gabby asked. "You're hibernating again."

"I know, it's been a while," he admitted and kissed her cheek, too. "But I'm here, right?"

"Only because it's a holiday," Muriel piped in. "Now shoo, unless you want to help cook. And if you see Ava, tell her she still has to mix this potato salad."

Rion told them, "Ava left, looking like a slutty Hello Kitty doll."

Muriel stopped cutting up vegetables and looked at Rion sharply. "Are you serious?"

"Let it go, Rel," Gabby said quietly.

"No, she's such a bitch!" their oldest sister yelled.

"It's fine, we got it," Gabby said.

Rion quietly left the kitchen, leaving his siblings to argue over Ava's lack of consideration. He spent time playing video games with the children until dinner was ready, then gathered them to sit at the table as Reese came in with his football.

Muriel yelled at her son, "Maurese, go right upstairs, wash up, and get back down here. You have five minutes!"

He ignored her. "Hey, Uncle Ree," he said first.

"Hey, Reese." He gave his nephew a dap and immediately noticed that he smelled like marijuana and his eyes were bloodshot. "You're good?"

"Yeah, I'm good."

"REESE!" Rion's sister yelled again.

"Alright, Ma, damn!" he yelled and went upstairs. Rion waited a few moments, then followed him. He didn't bother knocking. He just pushed open the bedroom door. Reese jumped back as he was coming out of his shirt.

"Damn, you scared the shit out of me, Unc!" he said, startled.

Rion got right to it. "You doing anything harder than weed?"

"What?"

"Don't play dumb with me," Rion said sternly. "You laced your weed with anything?"

"C'mon Unc," he said dismissively and turned around.

Rion stood in front of him. His fourteen year old nephew was tall for his age, the top of his head reaching Rion's shoulders. "You want to end up like Roslyn?"

"Yo, man—"

He tried to walk around. Rion got in his face and said again, "You see how she is when she's on that shit. You want to end up like her?"

"No, man!"

"Then answer my question."

"No, Unc, I ain't doing anything but weed," said Reese. "I know the deal."

"Okay," Rion said, backing off a bit. "You know I love you, right? Your mom, too. She loves the shit out of you. And you know we have a genetic disposition for addiction, so I need you to take it seriously. No pills, no X, no Molly, no heroin, no crack, no coke, no syrup, nothing."

"Iight Unc, I hear you." Rion didn't budge. "I hear you, Unc," he said more forcefully.

Rion grabbed his nephew and held him tight to his chest. At first, Reese didn't hug back, but then he decided to. Rion kissed the top of his head and left the room. Other than Ava, who used drugs to self-medicate her mental illness, they had all pretty much stayed away from all kinds of hard substances. Muriel only drinks occasionally and never touched drugs, Gabby doesn't drink or use at all, and Rion was under prescription by a doctor for his CBD, so he knew his limits. The last thing he needed was the next generation of the children of Roslyn going down the same path.

As the family ate their Thanksgiving dinner, Roslyn continued to try to talk to her son. "How's work, Ree? Is the new story coming out well?"

"It's fine," he said and turned to his sister, Ava, who had her face in her phone. "What are you watching?"

"A sex tape," she said casually.

"Avalon!" Gabby yelled at her.

"Whaaat? It's not mine," she said, still watching.

"That's a shock," Muriel murmured. "It's not like you don't have a couple out there already."

"Fuck you!" Ava yelled at her across the table.

"No, fuck you!" Muriel yelled back, still upset with Ava's disappearing act earlier in the day.

"No, fuck you!" Ava yelled again.

"No, fuck—"

"HEY!" their mother yelled. "Can we just have one day without the kids hearing you all yell and curse at each other?"

"Or talking about sex tapes?" Gabby added.

"I'm fine hearing about sex tapes," Reese said gleefully.

"Boy!" Muriel reached over and gently slapped her son on the back of his head.

"You see, Avalon!" Gabby yelled again.

"Ugh, fine, whatever," she said with an attitude and put her phone down.

They were quiet until Roslyn said, "I want you all to know how thankful I am for you. I'm a week away from getting my three-year chip, and it's because of you all, my children and my grandchildren give me the strength to go on. So thank you for never giving up on me, for always believing in me, and for standing by me all these years. I feel good about my ability to do things like make Thanksgiving dinner with my family." Tears began to fall out of her eyes.

"We love you, Mama," Gabby said and reached across the table to hold her hand. "We're always going to be rooting for you."

"Thank you, Gabby," she said to her youngest daughter.

"Yeah, we got your back, Mama," Ava said.

"Thank you so much, Ava," she said.

Muriel and Rion stayed quiet. Gabby hit his thigh under the table, and he flinched, then narrowed his eyes at her. There was no way he was going to applaud her for finally being a mother.

Muriel eventually said, "It's good news, Roslyn. I acknowledge that you're doing much better."

"Thank you so much, Rel," she responded.

Everyone turned to look at Rion. "Pass the mac and cheese, please," he said to his mother. Her eyes pooled with tears again, but she passed him the dish. "Thank you, Roslyn," he said politely.

Gabby whispered his name, "Rion!"

"Let it go, Gabbs," Muriel said. "Ree does not have to accept her amends."

"But—"

"It's fine, Gabrielle," Roslyn said. "Rion?" she called to him. Rion turned his face to her, looking bored. "I know you feel like I put you through a lot. But I'm glad that you're here. That's a step in the right direction for us."

Rion was trying really hard to keep it together, but her sweet-talking voice was too much.

"I don't *feel* like you put me through a lot, Roslyn. You *did* put me through a lot. Or did you forget that I was born with cocaine in my system? Or about selling all our goddamn stuff before I was old enough to speak to feed your heroin habit? Or maybe you forgot when you left me and Gabby alone with your drug-dealing boyfriend for two months, and we had no idea if you were alive or dead. Or maybe it was losing five different places to live because you just had to get your next fix. Or maybe it was getting the courts to drag us out of Maurese's house, only to turn around and start shooting up again. I did go through a lot. We all did. Muriel's looking for love in all the wrong places,

Ava is a fucking mental case, and Gabby pretends to have it all together, but one wrong move and she'll be shooting up her post office. And me? I'm an anxious-avoidant adult who struggles between wanting closeness and pushing people away at the same time that uses CBD to sleep most nights. So excuse me if your fortieth attempt to be a mother is something you think we should all jump for joy about."

Roslyn's tears continued to flow, but she said calmly, "I'm sorry, Rion. I really and truly am. And I'll spend the rest of my life making it up to you. Just tell me what you need from me."

He nodded. "Who's my father?"

The color drained from her face, and she immediately turned away to wipe her tears. "I told you I don't know."

He shook his head. "See, I don't believe that. Even in your highest of states, you knew who Maurese Hollingsworth was, you knew who Danny Santos was, and you knew who Gabriel Hernandez was. But you don't know who you named me after? An uncommon name like Rion?"

"Can we not do this today?" Muriel asked with a loud sigh.

"Fine. Can we also not pretend like she's going to stay clean?" Rion said to his oldest sister nastily and got up from the table.

"Jesus, Mama, you just had to push him, didn't you?" he heard Ava say.

Rion plopped on the living room couch and closed his eyes. Nick's face immediately popped into his head, like it always did when his eyes were closed. He wondered how he was spending his Thanksgiving. Probably with Penny at his childhood home in Rochester, New York, eating roasted duck instead of turkey. He felt the chair sink next to him.

"Leave me alone, Gabby," he said.

"Wrong sister," Ava said.

Rion opened his eyes and smiled at her. His Asian sister was the color of raw peanut butter, with shapely lips and brown eyes like his, but hers were more almond-shaped. He always thought she was beautiful without makeup, even if she didn't always see the beauty in herself. Her father, a half-white, half-Filipino businessman, lived in L.A. with his actual wife and children. But he had sent child support for her, five hundred dollars a month, until she turned eighteen years old. Most of it went to Roslyn's addiction. When Ava went to meet him on her nineteenth birthday, he pretended like he did not know who she was, so she attempted to burn down his house with him and his wife in it. That resulted in her second stint in a psych ward. While he considered Gabby his best friend, and Muriel a mother figure, Ava was the sister his brotherly nature came out for the most.

He put his head on her shoulder. "I'm not going to apologize," he said.

"I don't really give a shit," she replied in a bored manner. She reopened her phone. "Wanna watch this sex tape with me, baby bro?"

He chuckled. "Why are you so obsessed with this tape?"

"Because the whole tape was finally released. It's the singer, Kierra. The pictures came out weeks ago, but someone leaked the video online."

"Wow, really?"

"Yes! It's spicy as fuck. She's cute, but the guy is so hot."

"Yeah?"

Rion looked over as the cameraman showed Kierra on her back on a table, her black leather skirt hiked up to her stomach, her brown curly hair spread out, moaning loudly as a man between her legs pumped into her. Something about the way he moved was familiar to Rion. His pants were down, and his shirt was half hanging off his shoulders as he held one hand on her waist and the other on her small breasts. Rion's eyes narrowed, and he looked at the large labyrinth tattoo spread across the man's right shoulder and back...

His eyes went wide. "Holy, holy SHIT!" Rion yelled.

Rion snatched his sister's phone out of her hands and stood up quickly. "Hey!" she yelled. "I was—"

But he silenced her by putting his hand in her face and saying, "Shhhhhhhhh!!! I need to think!"

*It can't possibly be Nicholas ... right?* he asked himself, but his head already knew the answer.

He used his finger and pulled the dial all the way to the beginning of the video. He watched them kiss; his dirty blond hair slicked back, but it was from an angle, so he wasn't sure. Not until the man lifted her up and turned her around, his face in full view of the camera, before he plopped her onto the table and bent down to lift up her dress and slide down her thong.

"Nick!" he yelled.

"Yeah, you heard of him? His name is Nicholas Highton. Some rich playboy she performed at his family's masquerade ball on Halloween. He apparently got engaged that same night. Ain't that crazy!? Then, like an hour later, he was caught banging Kierra in a sunroom while the girlfriend celebrated their engagement. Kierra and the ex-fiancée got into a Twitter fight three weeks ago over it. She was calling her behavior classless, and Kierra called her assless. It was hilarious."

"Oh ... my ... God. Nicholas," Rion said again, in complete shock.

Ava took that opportunity to grab her phone back. "This has been going on for like a month. Where have you been? Oh, right, hibernating." She sat back down and continued to watch the video.

Rion pulled out his phone to call Nick, and remembered he had blocked his number. If he opened up that door, he knew he would not be able to resist walking through it fully. His manuscript was not done, and Nick's life was obviously messy right now. Rion reentering his life would just complicate it, making it even more messy.

"Ugh," Rion groaned.

He went upstairs to his sister's bedroom and turned on her computer. He put Nicholas Highton in the search bar, and all the articles and pictures came popping up on the screen. He was famous. More like infamous. The rich playboy who cheated on his fiancée with the singer Kierra right after the announcement of their engagement. Sixteen other women came out discussing their sexual encounters with him in various articles, four in the two years that he was supposedly with Penelope Benson. Nick's online magazine, Deep Strokez, also came up because the hashtag MrDeepStrokez had been trending on Twitter for weeks. All the publicity was making people pay attention to his magazine. So much so that it wasn't possible to order hard copies anymore; it was sold out on the site. And the website was most likely getting a ton of traffic, especially since he had one of his top reporters do an exclusive interview a week ago about what happened. It was an hour-long, Oprah-like interview in which he discussed his life from childhood all the way up to the incident. The only place you could see it was on his website.

Rion watched it with his mouth half open. With one incident, he had ended it with Penny, pissed his mother off, revealed his bisexuality in a public interview, and propelled his online magazine to a best seller.

"Holy, holy shit," Rion breathed out again.

"Thanks for watching her tonight, Ree," Gabby said as she took off her coat. "Was she good?"

"She's always good for me," Rion responded as he stretched out on the couch in his sister's apartment. "She fell asleep about an hour ago."

"Well, lately she's been Miss Sassy Pants, and I've had to remind her that she's not the boss. I am."

Gabrielle took off her shoes and attempted to sit on the couch. Rion lifted up his legs, and when she was seated, he put them down on her lap. His Hispanic sister also had full lips, but her brown hair was straight like their mother's. She was also the shortest of them all at 5'4". Gabby's skin was as light as his, but she browned in the sun more than Rion did.

"You look real pretty, sis," he said sincerely.

"Yeah, well, I'm trying to snag a husband," she said sarcastically.

He laughed a little. "How was it?"

"It was fine. Just a Christmas party with co-workers, nothing special."

"Yeah? Was Gael there?" he asked with a smile.

"Shut up," she told her brother. "Nothing is happening there. He's too old for me, and he doesn't know that I'm a single mom yet. That will have him running for the hills once he finds out."

"He's thirty-six, single, no kids, and likes you. I say give it a chance."

She shrugged. "Let's see if he makes a move," she said as she got comfortable. "And what about you? You and Jason still playing hide the eggplant?"

Normally it would have made him laugh, but instead, Rion said to her seriously, "I have a problem."

"What's going on? Something with Jay?"

"No, nothing with Jason. We broke up, for real this time, back in September."

"Uh-huh," she said skeptically.

"No, I'm not kidding, Gabbs. Remember my fling in London, Nicky?"

"The guy from New York? Yeah, what about him?"

He paused, then told her, "You know this whole Kierra scandal?"

She sat up straighter. "You are not going to tell me what I think you're going to tell me." He nodded with wide eyes. "Nicholas Highton? Mr. Deep Strokez himself is your Nicky!?"

"The very same," Rion confirmed.

"Holy, holy shit!" she yelled and jumped up.

"Shhhh! Don't wake Morgan. Did you drink tonight, sis?"

She grimaced. "No, of course not." She sat back down and moved closer. "So, what's the problem? Has he reached out?"

"No, he hasn't. And if he has, I wouldn't know because I blocked him."

"Whyyyy?" she whined.

"Because we can't be together. Or at least... I thought we couldn't. See my problem?"

Gabby nodded her head and said, "No."

Rion chuckled. "Did you watch the interview on his website?"

"No. Why?"

"Come watch it with me. I've watched it a million times since Thanksgiving." He pulled out his phone, and it immediately came up.

Rion and Gabby watched Nicholas talk about his family with baby pictures in the background. "I love my parents. I owe everything I am to them. They taught me to be strong, to stand by my beliefs, and to admit when you're wrong, but never be sorry for who you are. They inspire me to be exactly who I am today. The love and support they have given me over the years is indescribable."

"He fucking hates his parents, Gabbs," Rion told his sister. "They have given him neither love nor support. That was a dig at them."

Nick talked about his magazine and how it was his passion. "It's not just about sex stories. It's bringing real issues to light. We tackle taboo topics because people want to know about them. And we have a whole section educating others on various sex topics. We're not just giving you gossip; we're reporting the news, just like this report we're doing right now."

The reporter, Eddie Evans, asked about his relationship with Penelope, and Nick talked about them growing up together and then growing apart. "She is a beautiful, amazing, perfect woman that is going to make some man very happy one day. I'm just incredibly sad that it's not me. And I am deeply sorry that I've hurt her with all this. She deserves better than me."

When he smiled at the camera, Rion said to Gabby, "He's officially done with her. He's incredibly happy that he isn't engaged anymore, but he's softening the blow for her reputation."

"And he's officially single," Gabby said with an eyebrow raised.

"I'm going to get to that!" Rion said excitedly. "Keep watching!"

Nick talked about his interest in Buddhism. "I'm not exactly Buddhist, at least not yet. I still have a lot of learning and growing to do, but I do try to live my life with a few principles, such as mindfulness and living in the here and now. Being able to see what's right in front of me, enjoying the moment, and not be so consumed with what happens next."

"And was that what you did with Kierra?"

"Kierra and I were passing ships in the night, nothing more and nothing less. We were drawn to each other and fell into our desires. If I had known it was going to be recorded, I would have taken more precautions to protect her. But that is my only regret. There is nothing wrong with her being a sexually liberated woman and for me to express my sexual interest in her. We are human, sexual beings, primates. We need connections, even if it's just for the moment. But I didn't use her and throw her away. If she ever needs anything from me, I will be there for her because we made that connection. And if she never reaches out again, it's okay. She's a beautiful soul, and I wish her well."

"So you believe in giving into your desires with just about anyone?" Eddie asked.

"No. Not just anyone," Nick said. "With whoever comes across my path that I have a connection with. I know people are saying that I'm a playboy, but I'm not. I don't just sleep around. It has to be real and meaningful, even if it is just for a short time. I met someone when I was in London back in June, and we had an amazing connection. A life-changing one that meant everything to me, even if they don't feel the same about me." Nick turned to the camera and said, "I will never forget you and what we had in London."

Gabby's mouth dropped, and she turned to her brother, who was watching the interview intently. She turned back to the screen as the reporter asked, "And you're not going to tell the world who this very important woman is that changed your life?"

Nick shook his head, "No." He took a moment and said, "He knows who he is."

Gabby gasped. "Did he just come out!?" She started hitting her brother's arm with every word. "Did. He. Just. Come. Out!?"

"Stop hitting me!" he yelled, then hushed her. "Shhh! You missed the part!" He rewound the video a few seconds.

"...saying that you're also connecting with... men?" They could tell the reporter, his own employee, was surprised.

"That I'm bisexual, yes. Or maybe I'm just a demi-sexual that's attracted to the connection regardless of genitals? I don't know. Does it matter? In the illustrious words of David Schitt, 'I'm into the wine and not just the label,'" he said with a smile. "But I doubt I will sleep with another man again for a long time. No one else compares to him. And no, I don't just mean sexually. Life is about connections, and we created a strong one in less than a week. One that had me back on a plane a few days later just to spend the rest of the month with him in his arms. You don't just connect on the level that we did and walk away to try to recreate that with someone else. At least I don't."

"Rion!" Gabby yelled again. "He thinks you don't care about him!"

"I know!" Rion said painfully. "I don't know what to do."

She spun him around. "Yes, you do, Ree. Yes. You. Do." Rion looked at his sister with fear in his eyes. Gabby paused the video. "Rion, he just told the entire world that you meant everything to him, but he thinks you don't give a shit about him! He just came out to the entire world because of you! Confessed how deeply he fell for you, dammit! And you're not going to take that as an opening to go get him back!?"

"Was that an opening, though?" Rion asked. "I don't know if that was an opening... or a goodbye. See my problem?"

"Well, the only way you're going to know is if you swallow your pride and go to him," she said.

"I gotta get on a plane, though," he whined.

"Rion Daniel Matthews!" his sister shrieked and stood up. She pointed a finger in his face and yelled,

"If you don't get your sorry, white ass on the next plane to JFK—"

"Mama?"

They both looked over to see Morgan rubbing her eyes and looking confused. "What time is it, Mama?"

"I'm so sorry, baby!" Gabby said, running to her daughter and hugging her. "You're Uncle Ree is being an idiot, so Mama was yelling at him, but I'll keep it down now. Let me go tuck you in."

Gabby turned her around and followed her daughter back to her bedroom. Rion sighed and listened to the rest of the interview. There was no more talk about his sexuality, only his work with the magazine, pictures of his apartment overlooking the Hudson River, and his favorite things, like his tuxedo cat Izzy. Rion put it on mute and looked at him, the way his blue button-down shirt fit his body, along with his tan khakis and leather boots. His hair was getting long, and his facial hair was growing in, making him look older, more mature, sexier.

"I'm so incredibly fucked," he said to himself.

Gabby came back out a few minutes later and sat on the couch next to him. They sat in silence for a moment, then she asked, "Do you still care about him?"

"So much it hurts to think about him," he murmured.

"Do you want to see him?"

"So badly."

"What do you think will happen if you go to him?"

"Knowing Nick?" Rion shrugged. "He'll be pissed that I ghosted him. He'll either pretend like he doesn't give a shit, or he'll coldly send me away. He's too cool for it to be a scene."

"So you don't think he'll want to be with you?"

"I... I don't know," Rion answered honestly.

"But what if he does, Ree? What if he wants that connection you had back? What if it never left for him like it never left for you?"

"How would that even work, Gabbs? We live in different states, different time zones. I'm not getting on a plane to go see him every couple of weeks, and I can't expect him to do the same for me."

"Then I guess you're gonna have to stay in New York," she said casually. He turned his head and looked at her. "You have no ties here, Rion. You don't need that bookstore job anymore; you're a writer that gets paid for writing. And you can write from anywhere."

"What do you mean? I have you!" he said to her forcefully. "And Ava and Muriel and the kids... I can't just leave you all behind."

"You can. And you will." Gabby took his hands in hers. "I am fine. I have a steady job, and I can take care of Morgan just fine. Muriel is fine. She's been taking care of her children just fine without you and will continue to. Even Ava, now that she is on meds, is fine. And Roslyn is clean. And even if she wasn't, she can't hurt us anymore with her drug addiction because we're adults now. So the only thing keeping you here is your fear of being rejected. And your fear of flying."

He sighed. "And if he does reject me?"

She squeezed his hands. "Then you'll come back here and write. Or you'll move to London and write there. But either way, you won't regret putting your heart out there."

He leaned in and put his head on his smaller sister's shoulder. She let go of one of his hands and rubbed his neck. "But he's not going to reject you, baby bro," she said softly. "Not that man who told the whole world that meeting you was life-changing for him, that he'll never forget you, that he won't be sleeping with men for a while because of what the two of you shared. He loves you, too."

"I didn't say that I loved him," Rion murmured from her shoulder.

"You didn't have to. And neither did he," Gabby said back. She kissed the side of his head. "You going home or staying here tonight?"

"I'm here. I promised Morgan I'd make my Scary Pancakes before she goes to school."

"Ah, the famous Uncle Ree's Scary Pancakes. The ones that are never shaped like a circle but globs of some alien-like creatures."

"The very same." He let a moment pass and said, "You smell nice. Did you dance with Gael tonight?"

Gabby smiled and pushed him off her. "Goodnight, Ree," she said as she stood up.

"Night, Gabbs. Thanks."

Gabby left Rion in the living room. Rion stretched out on the couch and put his arm over his head, reliving every moment of his time with Nick at the Mandarin Oriental.

*R*ion found himself sitting on his windowsill on Christmas night after spending the day at Muriel's house with his family. It was a quiet, clear sky, with only a few sounds of people walking past his building. Even the local bar on the corner was quiet. He had rolled a joint and began smoking, looking at the moon and thinking about Nicholas. Rion had one leg over the ledge of his fourth-floor apartment window, the other knee up, leaning back, listening to Glass Animals' *Heat Waves* on repeat.

Since Rion had submitted his manuscript officially two weeks ago, he had nothing to occupy his time, so he used it to make up a fake social media profile and stalked Nick on all of his social media accounts. He had been scrolling through Nick's Instagram page and found out it had been more active in the last two months than it had been in the last two years. Rion suspected that someone from his team was monitoring it, taking over the weekly posting of pictures and quotes from the magazine. Using his fame to promote his work was genius, he had to admit. He was also happy to see his model-like pictures: bare-chested, pictures of him in full suits, selfies of him and his cat.

Nick had been seen in the company of Kierra after the incident at a public dinner that was obviously staged for the paparazzi. He was also rumored to be linked with an Argentinian supermodel, Yesenia Cortez, for the last month, who was his date to a Christmas event at Rockefeller Center two days ago. He was becoming elusive and mysterious to the tabloids, so they made up stuff about him. *The Sun* had stated that his London lover was none other than his best friend, Parker Madison.

Parker cleared that up right away in an interview, saying cheekily, "If I had wanted to be Nicholas's life-changing, sexual soulmate, I would have done it our sophomore year in college. But, bullocks, his cock is too big for my tastes." That made Rion laugh out loud.

Since Nick's tryst had made international news, and everyone assumed his lover was English, Rion welcomed calls from Kaleb, Sonny, and even Lennox, who all knew who Nick was referring to but did not dare go to the tabloids. It was a code they shared; since Nick didn't say his name, they weren't going to either. But Kaleb said, "I told you the universe was going to find a way to push you back together, mate. So what's your plan?"

By that time, Rion was less afraid of getting on a plane and more afraid of what Nick would say if he walked back into his life. He wasn't even sure what he would want from Nick... a friendship? Friends with benefits? A relationship? He just knew he needed to see him. To see if his words still held up, that if they were ever in the same place, the same space, that Nick would always want to be with him. Rion knew it was still true for him but expanded: As long as they were on the same continent, same globe, Rion would want Nicholas in his life.

By the time the joint was finished, Rion had made up his mind. He opened his laptop and looked up the next flight from SFO to JFK, non-stop, to avoid having to go up in the air twice this time.

As soon as Rion got off the elevator on the 34th floor, the glass wall and doors were in front of him. He opened the door with the logo Deep Strokez Media and Publications on it. It was an open floor plan: a large counter desk right up front and desks behind it turned any way they wanted to. Some people were typing, some were talking, and one guy was taking a nap on the couch near the window. There was a large conference room table right in the middle of the room that could seat at least twenty people and an office with the door wide open all the way in the back.

Rion stopped at the counter. "Hello. Is Nicholas Highton available?"

"Do you have an appointment?" the woman asked.

"Erm... no."

She narrowed her eyes at him. "Are you the press?"

He shook his head. "No. A friend."

She opened up a green notebook and looked up. "He currently does not have any appointments at the moment, so I can tell him you're here and see if he is free."

She picked up the phone and dialed Nick's extension as Rion waited and looked around. Before she said the words, Rion had already spotted him. He was sprouting a full beard; the middle part of his hair was still longer than the sides, falling over his face. Seeing him again made him speechless for a moment.

"He's currently not in his office, but he may be on the floor." She stood up and looked around.

"He's over there." Rion pointed at Nick, leaning over a desk with someone going over a large computer screen. "Is it okay if I walk over?"

"I'll need you to sign in," the front desk clerk commanded. "Do you have ID?"

"Sure."

Rion pulled out his California state driver's license, handed it to her, and signed the book. She handed it back to him after comparing the name on his card to his name in the book and smiled.

"Go right in," she said.

Rion's heart started beating faster as he paused in front of the low swinging cafe doors. But then he found his nerve and walked through, straight to the desk Nick was leaning over.

Nick was in the middle of explaining which image would be better for the layout to the art designer when he sensed someone walking toward them. He looked up and locked eyes with Rion, and his breath caught in his throat for a moment. He slowly stood upon seeing his ex-lover, partly thinking somehow he was a mirage and partly stunned that he was actually there.

Rion spoke first. "Hi, Nick."

Nick stared for a moment before he found his voice. "What are you doing here?"

"Can we talk?" Rion asked, holding onto the strap of his book bag tightly.

"You're looking for a job?" Nick asked seriously.

Rion resisted the urge to roll his eyes. "No, Nick, I'm not looking for a job. Can we talk?" he asked again.

Nick looked around at his employees doing a bad job of minding their business. It was moments like this he regretted his flat organization structure. Everyone thought they had a right to know what was going on in his life, especially after the Kierra situation.

"Yeah," Nick answered him. "Come into my office."

Nick guided Rion to the room in the back of the space. Rion looked at the large wooden desk in front of a picture window of New York skyscrapers. Nick closed the door behind him and went to sit behind his desk.

"Wow, you really like views," said Rion.

"What can I do for you, Rion?" Nick asked formally.

Rion took notice of the coldness in his voice and received confirmation of how upset he was. Although it was expected, he couldn't help the hurt he felt. He decided to jump right in it.

Rion didn't sit, instead started talking. "I just wanted to come by and explain."

"Explain what?"

"Why I didn't return any of your calls and texts."

"You got on a plane and crossed the country just to explain why you didn't call me back?" Nick asked calmly.

"I know you're upset with me, Nick. I'm so, so sorry for ghosting you the last couple of months—"

"Five."

Rion was confused. "Five?"

"It's been five months."

"Oh." Rion was crestfallen. *Has it really been five months?* "Yeah, I guess it has. But listen, I just needed to stay focused and finish my manuscript by the deadline. Sometimes I get like that, just drawn into my work. But it's done; I finished the draft and sent it to my editor two weeks ago. So I'm back in the real world."

"That's wonderful," Nick said dryly.

"Yeah. And I'm doing the dedication to you. You're like... my muse," Rion said with a smile.

Nicholas did not smile back. "Was there something you wanted, Rion?"

Rion missed Nick calling him Ree. "Yes. That's not all I wanted to say." He stepped closer to his desk and spoke honestly.

"I know I hurt you, and I'm sorry. But you need to know that not a day went by when I didn't think about you a thousand times. Not a night has passed when I didn't dream about you. I needed to put some distance between us because my thoughts of you were consuming me; I couldn't eat, I couldn't sleep, and I couldn't work. And I needed to finish the project I had started. It wasn't until I was done that I let my feelings overwhelm me completely. I had to see you. And I know it's not fair of me to expect anything; you have a full life here, famous and busy and all. But I watched your interview. Probably a thousand times already. And I wanted to clear something up. I need you to know the tremendous impact you had on me, too. Being with you the entire month of June meant everything to me. You meant everything to me. It was real to me, everything we shared, everything we felt, and I have never forgotten either, and I never will. So

I just wanted to make sure you never doubted how I felt about you for one second. How I... How I still feel about you."

Nick's stoic face did not change. "Is that it?"

"Yeah. Yeah... that's... it." Rion felt his bravery waning.

"Okay."

"Okay... I guess I'll... erm... Bye, Nicholas."

"Bye, Rion," Nick responded without emotion.

Rion stared at him a bit longer, then turned around to leave, walking very slowly. Nick looked up at the ceiling, feeling his own resolve waning with every step Rion took to his door. By the time Rion put his hand on the doorknob, Nick said out loud, "Have dinner with me tonight."

Rion turned around with wide eyes. "Okay."

Nick looked down and stared at him. "And then stay the night with me."

"Okay," Rion responded.

"I'll text you the time and address."

"Okay. I have to unblock your number."

Nick grimaced and put his hand to his chest. "Ouch."

Rion looked horrified. "I'm sorry! I just ruined the moment, didn't I?" Nick finally cracked a smile. "Look, I'm doing it right now!" Rion took out his phone and began typing. Nick's phone buzzed on the desk, but he did not look at it. "I'll wait for your text with the time and place," said Rion.

"Okay," said Nick.

Rion turned to leave again and heard Nick say, "I still think about you a thousand times a day, too, Ree."

Rion turned around and smiled that smile that made Nick happy. He hit the door twice on his way out.

Nick sighed. He picked up his phone and read Rion's text:

[RWAWN2. Always.]

Rion looked up Mastro's Restaurant once he got the text to meet Nick there at 8 p.m., and he knew he had to dress up. He bought a five hundred dollar charcoal black suit with a gray shirt and black tie to look nice for Nick. He was especially nervous walking into an expensive restaurant, aware that his clothes were polyester and his shoes were indeed from Aldo's. Nick had never made him feel that way, but in London, it felt like they were on an equal footing. Now Rion felt like he was stepping into Nick's world, his home turf, so he needed to play the part to impress him.

Rion didn't want to be late, so he arrived ten minutes before the hour and said more confidently than he felt, "Good evening. I'm meeting Mr. Highton for dinner."

The host nodded. "Yes, Mr. Matthews, right this way."

Surprised that he knew his name, Rion followed the host to the right side of the restaurant to a square table by the bar. The host handed Rion a menu, put the other on the table across from him, and said, "Enjoy," before walking away.

He sat down and tried to look like he fit in. But he didn't have long to wait because five minutes later, he saw Nicholas coming toward him. He had changed from the jeans and button-down shirt that he had been wearing earlier in the day into a dark blue, pin-striped suit that looked expensive from where Rion was sitting. He wore a crisp white shirt and a blue and silver tie to match. Rion's heart beat faster with every step Nick took toward the table unable to take his eyes off of how gorgeous Nicholas was. He found himself standing up, straightening out his own tie, and trying to breathe very slowly.

Nick came to the table and nodded at him. "Rion."

"Hi, Nick," Rion said softly.

Nick gestured for Rion to sit, and he did. He cleared his throat and asked casually, "How was your flight?"

Rion chuckled. "I didn't throw up on the guy sitting next to me, so I guess I did okay."

"Yeah? Did you converse with another stranger on a plane?"

"Of course I did. It's the only way I know how to be."

"Great. What did you find out about them?" Nick asked as he leaned back with his hands folded.

"Well, he's originally from the area, and he hasn't been home in a while, so he scheduled a trip to see his parents. They live in... Queens? I think that's what he said. I don't know the difference, but it sounds like a nice place to live."

"Depends on which part," Nick spoke as the wait-ress came to the table. She introduced herself and explained the chef's specials for the evening. Nick said, "We'll start with the lobster roll and sea scallops while we decide on an entrée. And bring cabernet sauvignon for the table. Thank you." After she had left he turned back to Rion. "So you were saying?"

"No, you were saying... talking about... Queens..."

Rion felt himself losing it moment by moment as Nick seemed amazingly calm and collected. He regretted not taking an edible before dinner.

"Ah. Yes, Queens," Nick said. "There are some decent areas, especially the townships going toward the island."

"The Island?"

"Long Island. Brian lives on the Island, West Islip. The Hightons have a home in the Hamptons. Two actually, Montauk and Napeague. But the one in Napeague is a vacation rental throughout the year. One of my father's many properties. Montauk is the one my family actually stays in during the summer."

"Wow. Way to remind me how poor I am," Rion joked.

Nick smiled. Then he looked down at his fingers and asked, "Why are you here, Ree?"

"I told you why. I wanted you to know—"

"No," Nick said sharply, cutting him off. He looked up and stared at him. "You could have told me all that over the phone. Or in an *email*." Nick practically sneered, and Rion knew his email to Nick back in September really pissed him off. "Why are you here?" he asked again. Rion stared back and did not answer.

Nick sighed. "You are the most confusing human being on the face of the planet."

"What do you want me to say?" Rion asked in a low voice.

Nick leaned in and replied in a low voice, "I want you to stop saying one thing and doing another."

"I'm sorry," Rion said earnestly. "I'm sorry that I'm still sending you mixed messages. I'm sorry that I don't just know what I want, or even if I do know what

I want, how to just go for it. I learned a long time ago that just because you want something doesn't mean the universe will let you have it."

"Then why are you *here*?" Nick asked again, more forcefully than the last two times.

"Because I still want to be with you!" Rion blurted out, then gasped.

Nick's lips parted slightly, then curved into a smile. "That's all I wanted to know," he said softly. He sat back and asked, "How is your family? Your sisters, Gabby, Ava, and Muriel? And Morgan? Reese, Jeff, and... sorry I don't remember Muriel's daughter's name."

Rion's eyes were still wide at what he confessed. "Erm..." He looked around the restaurant as if others had heard him until his eyes landed back on Nick's blue ones. "Kate. They're fine. Everyone's fine."

"Yeah? What did you do for Christmas?" Nick asked as the appetizers were brought to the table and the wine was poured.

"Erm... Spent it with them and Roslyn at Muriel's house. We don't give each other gifts, a habit from when we were young and didn't have money to give gifts, but we make sure the children get three gifts each from all of us, so they always have a Christmas. That started when Reese was a baby."

"That's your oldest nephew, right? How old is he? Thirteen?" Nick started eating.

"Fourteen," Rion responded, still feeling vulnerable about telling Nick he wanted to be with him. He knew what Nick was trying to do, keeping things sociable between them, but Rion didn't want that. "Nick—"

"Nicky," Nick responded. "Only you can call me Nicky, so you should take advantage of it."

Rion smiled a little. "Nicky? What is it that you want? From me? From... us?"

Nick inhaled and exhaled deeply. "With you. Not from you. I don't want anything *from* you, Rion. I just wanted to know that you still cared about me because I still care about you. Because you're right, it hurt when you disappeared on me. I know we said we needed a clean break, but I never thought we'd actually take one. I thought... I don't know what I thought. I guess I thought I'd get to keep you in my life somehow. I guess I thought you wanted the same thing."

"I did. I *do*. I ... do."

"But...?" Nick encouraged. Rion didn't respond at first. "I need to know what I did to make you pull away from me," Nick said with a frown, his first sign of vulnerability.

"You didn't really do anything. It's just that... our worlds were colliding. When it was just the two of us in London, it felt like nothing could ever pull us apart. But then here, there were so many things... my work, your... Penny..."

"So, Penelope?" Nick confirmed. He had suspected it, but he needed to hear Rion say it. "You pulled away because of Penny in my life?"

"I couldn't bear the thought of you being with someone that wasn't me. Just thinking about you sleeping with her on the fourth... And that's not fair to you. I know that. You had a whole life before you met me and—"

"I didn't have a life before I met you, Rion," he broke into Rion's speech. "Not a personal one. Everything was a business transaction, including my relationship with Penny. I told you I needed to end it, and I did."

Rion gave him a look of disbelief. "Actually, what you did was blow up your life, and that had nothing to do with me. It could have gone very, very badly for you, but you're rich and handsome and got lucky." Rion didn't mean for it to come out snarky, but it did, and Nick heard it.

Nick lifted his chin up. "You're right. I did blow up my life. I was angry. I was angry at you for disappearing on me the way you did. I was angry at my mother and Penny for orchestrating a fake engagement an entire two months after I broke up with Penny face-to-face. I was angry at everyone pulling my life in the direction they thought it should go, and I wanted to take some of my power back. And, I might have been a little coked up." He shrugged.

Rion froze, then said, "So you sniff coke?"

Nick shrugged again. "Not really. But I did that night." Rion nodded and made a face that Nick couldn't place. "What was that for? I'm not a drug addict, Ree. You know that."

Rion shook his head. "Nothing. It's... nothing." He changed the subject. "So you broke up with Penny first?"

"In August."

"Wow. And they blindsided you by announcing your engagement to her when you weren't even a couple?"

"In front of five hundred of our closest friends, family members, and business associates," Nick said dryly.

"So you slept with Kierra on purpose? Filmed it on purpose? Just to piss everyone off?" Rion asked incredulously.

"I thought it was going to be a few pictures, not a whole sex tape," he said with another shrug.

Rion was dumbfounded. "Who the fuck are you, Nicholas?"

Nick leaned into the table again and looked him in the eyes. "I thought about you the whole time. I kept looking up at the moon and pretending I was inside of you. I almost called out your name at least three times." Rion was speechless, especially knowing he did the same when he was with Jason. "That's who I am, Rion. Someone who needed to be free, in case this," he gestured toward the two of them together, "were to ever happen. In the rare chance that our paths met at a crossroads again, I wanted to make sure I was completely available for you, even if that meant that I had nothing else. So maybe I did blow up my life. But if the end result was us being together, I'd blow it up a thousand more times just to be with you."

Rion could feel his heart burst with love for Nick. "That was very poetic of you, Nicky," he teased.

"It's the truth." They stared at each other until Nick spoke again. "So. Is this happening?"

Rion almost yelled, "Yes!" but then he swallowed. "I want to... but... aren't you still seeing Yesenia? You were together just five days ago, so you aren't exactly available." Nick didn't answer, but he also didn't look away. "Are you sleeping with her?" he asked in an accusing tone.

"Yes. Did you sleep with Jason?" Nick asked calmly.

Rion hesitated, then said, "Yes."

"Hmm. Is it over?" Nick asked in the same tone of voice.

"Yes. For good."

"Okay," Nick said. He picked up his fork and poked at a scallop. "Try the sushi here. It's wonderful."

"Nick—" Rion began.

But Nicholas cut him off. "Are you going to dwell on the things we did when we were not together, or are you going to build on what we have and grow it? Because if you're not going to do that, then again, I ask, why did you come?"

Rion was speechless. Nick continued, "By tomorrow morning, you will need to have made a decision. We can be friends. Or we can be something greater. Or we can walk away and never meet again. But it has to be resolved before the sun rises tomorrow."

"I don't like the Nicholas in front of me," Rion said. "The Nicky I met showed me that he cared about me and didn't give me ultimatums. What happened to 'no pressure?'"

Nick let a moment pass. "The Nicky you met put his heart on the table more than once for you. You're asking me to do that again with no assurances that you're going to stay with me?"

Rion was again left speechless, but then he was honest. "I was... scared, Nicholas. I'm still scared. I've never felt this way about anyone before."

Nick nodded. "Well, try the bone-in Kansas strip steak. Maybe that will lessen your fears about being with me." He continued eating, glancing up at Rion with a smirk.

Rion found himself smiling. He picked up a fork and began to eat, too. "How is Izzy? You never mentioned you have a cat."

Nick smiled back. "You never asked. Izzy is five years old and the only female that is allowed to stay the night at my house."

They began talking casually, discussing the holidays they missed, and updating each other on family news. Rion caught Nick up on his manuscript and what's been going on with their friends in London. Nick caught him up on how his behavior made his magazine more famous than ever before. Rion confessed to stalking him on Instagram, making him laugh, and Nick admitted that Marcel handled his social media pages, but he had the final say on the pictures. The Kansas steak was perfect to Rion, just like the night was. While it had started off tense, by the end of the night, they were both more relaxed and enjoying the company, like old times.

While drinking wine and eating their butter cake, a woman came to the table and touched Nick's shoulder. "Hi, I'm Vivian. I wanted to come over and introduce myself."

Nick stood up and shook her hand. "Hello, Vivian."

"I just wanted to tell you that my friends and I," she pointed at the table of three more women, "we really appreciate your magazine, your platform, and your voice, empowering women to be sexually liberating. It's so inspiring." She stood there holding onto his hand and looking dreamily into his eyes.

"Thank you. I'm glad to have helped in any way," he said politely.

She continued to stare at him for an uncomfortable moment until she said, "So, I'm curious, do you feel an instant connection with me? Because I can feel it with you." She stared at him longingly.

Rion couldn't help it. He snorted in laughter before he caught himself. They both turned to look at him. Vivian's eyes were cold as she looked down on him; Nick's eyes were full of amusement.

Nick turned back to her. "I'm sorry. I don't feel an instant connection. That's not to say you're not a beautiful woman. You're very beautiful. But I get the sense that you are still occupied."

Her eyes went wide. "How did you know?"

"Call it intuition," he said with a wink. "I would love to meet your friends if you want to introduce me to them. Rion, you don't mind, do you?" He winked at Rion as well.

"Not at all, Nicholas. Please, go adorn your fans." Rion winked back.

Rion watched Nick walk over to the table, and the rest of the women's eyes sparkled with excitement. He watched them gush all over him and take pictures, individually and together. He thought about Nick's personality and how he was accustomed to getting everything he wanted. And what he wanted was Rion. Not Penny, or Kierra, or Yesenia, or any of the women at the table. That made him smile.

When Nick came back to the table, Rion asked, "Is it fun? Being recognized everywhere you go, Mr. Deep Strokez?"

"It's a little fun," Nick admitted. "I get a lot of *that*, people asking me about connections. Men and women now. That's the fun part."

"Do you have a connection with Yesenia?"

Nick tried not to smile. "Yes. A sexual one only. When her brown hair is wet, it gets curly and matted to her face, like yours. It helps me to pretend that it's you." Rion felt his face flush, but didn't respond. "She doesn't want to be with someone. Her career is the most important thing to her, and being seen with me is good for her career. But this arrangement is on my terms, Ree. I can end it anytime."

That definitely made Rion happy to hear. "And how does Madeline feel about it? Your own confessed sexual liberation? Your bisexuality?"

"I have no idea," Nick said with a shake of his head. "I haven't spoken to Madeline since the Masquerade Gala. She typically calls me every Friday, but she didn't the following Friday or the Friday after that. I tried calling her, but it goes straight to voicemail. Emma said she is still deciding what to do with me."

"Wow." Parker's words about either being hidden from them or destroying Nick's fragile relationship with his family came back to Rion. He said to Nick, "If we do this, I don't want them to know that we're together, Nicholas."

Nick cocked his head to the side in confusion. "Who? My parents?"

"Yeah. It's already so fragile. Throwing me in their face will just complicate things more. In fact," he took a deep breath and said, "I don't want the world to know either. I'd rather be your little secret than end up in the tabloids."

Nick shook his head. "I'm not hiding you, Rion. If we're together—"

Rion reached over and touched his hand. "I'm asking to be hidden. Even Oprah hid Stedman for a long time before people knew there was a Stedman, and she's still mums about it. I can be your Stedman."

Nick chuckled. "That's the sweetest and weirdest thing anyone has ever said to me." Rion smiled at him. "I guess I have some decisions to make, too. Can I think it over?"

"Of course. We have until the sun rises, right?" Rion said.

"Right." Nick stroked his fingers. "You're ready to go home?" he asked.

Rion was surprised. "You're taking me to your sanctuary?"

Nick kept a straight face and said, "Well, I thought about a back alley, but since you wore a suit, I figured I could at least give you a warm bed to sleep in tonight."

"I feel special," Rion said sarcastically.

"You're going to feel more than just special, Ree. You're going to feel everything I feel for you," Nick said in a low and seductive voice. "Would you like that?"

Rion felt his pants tighten on his thigh. "I would like that very much," he said softly.

"Thank you for consenting," Nick said. "Now, let's go."

They didn't talk again. Nick kept his eyes on Rion and raised his finger. The waitress came, and Nick gave her his card. They waited until the check was paid, then Nick stood up. Rion stood up as well and followed him out of the restaurant. Nick gave his ticket to the valet, and Rion stood there, taking in the sights and sounds of New York City as they waited. Suddenly, a dark blue Audi R8 Spyder stopped in front of them. The valet left the door open for Nick as he approached.

Rion was in awe. "You're shitting me!"

Nick smiled. "I shit you not. Get in."

Rion slipped into the passenger side, and Nick pulled out of the space. They drove out of the lot and took Sixth Ave to his apartment on Riverside Boulevard. Nick drove fast, weaving in and out of traffic, exhilarating Rion. As he was waiting at a light, he looked over at Rion's face, only lit up by the streetlights. He still couldn't believe Rion was there, that he had actually gotten on a plane to come to him. He didn't know what would happen tomorrow, but he was grateful to the universe for bringing Rion back to him. Nick felt the strongest urge to pull his face toward him and kiss him. Rion must have sensed him because he slowly turned his head and locked eyes with Nick. A moment before Nick was about to lean in, the car behind him honked. Rion's face broke into a wide smile.

Nick groaned in his throat and pulled off, his tires screeching across the tar road. He continued to drive, thinking of all the things he was going to do to Rion the moment he closed his door when he felt a hand on his thigh, a squeeze, then felt it move to the crease at his groin. He did not look down, keeping his eyes on the road as Rion's hand moved farther in, gently cupping his penis on his inner thigh, rubbing it back and forth.

"I called out your name when I was with Jason," Rion confessed. "I thought about you the whole time, too. I closed my eyes and pretended I was inside of you, and I called out your name when I came. And I don't regret it."

"Wow," Nick said quietly. That confession made him very happy.

Rion kept rubbing. Nick tried very hard to concentrate on the road but almost missed his turn, so he pressed his brakes and screeched again, and did a wide turn into the block.

Rion's right hand instinctively reached up and held the roof of the car. "Whoa!"

"Sorry. I was... distracted," Nick said, his eyes still on the road. Rion smiled without looking at him.

When they pulled up to the building, Nick left his keys in the car and got out. Rion was confused but followed him. "Thaddeus," he called out. "Please call the valet."

"Right away, Mr. Highton. Good evening," the doorman responded as he held the door open for them.

"Of course, you have a doorman. And a valet," Rion whispered.

"And a 24-hour concierge," Nick whispered back, and winked. Rion rolled his eyes but smiled back.

They entered the elevator together, and Nick kept his face neutral, trying to control his excitement. He glanced at Rion from the corner of his eye, who was having a harder time hiding his feelings on his face, and it almost made him smile. They took the elevator to the 19th floor in silence. Nick sensed Rion glancing at him from time to time. They stepped off and walked down the hall to Nick's corner apartment, and he opened the door.

"Holy, holy shit," he heard Rion say quietly.

Rion stepped into the large, high-ceilinged condo. It was clean and styled contemporarily. He passed the kitchen island and through the living room with a brown leather couch with a sixty-inch flat screen across from it. The only light in the room was from a small lamp that displayed a soft yellow glow. Rion walked straight to the wall of windows overlooking the Hudson River.

"You really like views," he said to Nick.

Nick walked up and stood directly behind him, pressing his groin against Rion's bottom and wrapping his hands around his waist. "I'm not interested in the views right now," he said softly.

He reached up to Rion's shoulders and slid off his suit jacket, tossing it onto his leather couch. Nick felt

Rion's breath become labored as he pulled his shirt out from his pants along with his t-shirt and began to rub his hard abs up to his nipples and back down. Nick kissed the back of Rion's neck, sucked and nibbled on his earlobe, putting his tongue in Rion's ear.

"I missed you so much, Ree," he murmured. "Did you miss me?"

Rion turned around and said, "A thousand times a day." He grabbed the back of Nick's neck and smashed their lips together.

Nick growled and pushed him against the glass. They kissed aggressively, teeth clashing, lips biting. Rion managed to get Nick's suit jacket off and was working on his tie when Nick suddenly dropped to his knees. Rion ran his hands through Nick's hair while Nick anxiously unbuckled Rion's belt and popped the button off his suit pants, yanking them down with his boxer briefs.

Rion gasped at the feel of Nick's beard rubbing against his genitals, the tickling sensation making him instantly hard. Nick continued to be aggressive, stroking Rion a few times before his long tongue came out, and he licked the pre-cum off his cock head like an ice cream cone. Even in the dim light, he could see Nick's blue eyes, wanting, needing him. Rion reached down and caressed his face.

Nick looked up at Rion and opened his mouth wide. He put Rion in his mouth and sucked gently. Rion moaned. Nick leaned back slightly and opened up his throat, pushing Rion to him and farther in his mouth. Rion obliged, putting his seven and a half inches farther and farther down until the hair on Nick's chin brushed against the hair on Rion's testicles. Then he slowly slid out, Nick's phlegmy saliva coating Rion's cock, dripping from the head and his mouth.

"Oh my God, you're so good at this, too," Rion whispered. "Do it again, please?"

Nick did, and Rion held onto Nick's shoulders as he entered his mouth fully, but didn't slide all the way out, only halfway, then back down Nick's throat again. He slowly pumped into Nick's face, moaning softly, and Nick held onto Rion's thighs and allowed it. Suddenly, he pulled out.

"Fuck, I almost came down your throat," he said breathlessly.

"Hmmm," Nick responded, then began to stroke and suck Rion with fervor.

Rion closed his eyes and allowed his mind to go blank and his orgasm to take over. He didn't have time to tell him. His balls tightened and released thick and warm cum into Nick's mouth. Nick did not stop sucking until Rion whimpered and fell over him, completely spent from the simple act of fellatio, his pants still stuck at his ankles.

Rion laid on the floor laughing. Nick smiled, leaned over, and kissed his lips. "Your shoes are nice. Now take them off, along with the rest of your clothes. Meet me in the bedroom," he said and stood up. He left Rion on the floor in the living room.

"I don't know where the bedroom is," Rion called out.

"You'll figure it out," Nick responded from somewhere in the fourteen hundred square foot apartment.

Rion turned onto his back and laid on the floor, his pants still down at his ankles, the happiest he had been in five months. He felt the brush of fur at his side and looked down to see Izzy had come out from under the couch and rubbed against him. He stroked her head a few times until she purred. Then he stood up and took off his clothes, taking his time.

Rion left them on the living room floor then went toward the front of the home and found the hallway leading to the bedrooms. He opened the first door, and it was a bathroom. The second door was a bedroom with a desk in it, but it was empty. The third door was a laundry room. At the end of the hall were double doors. He opened them gently. In front of him was a huge walk-in closet. He looked to the right and there was a large master bath. He looked to the left, and there was Nicholas on his king-size bed surrounded by pillows, naked, waiting for him. The room was lit with several tea-light candles, just enough light to see him. The sheets were burgundy colored silk, and the comforter was burgundy and gold, pulled back to the side. A bottle of Pjur and two condoms were on a pillow next to him.

Rion came over to the edge of the bed and asked softly, "May I?"

"Yes," Nick replied softly. "Yes, you may."

Rion crawled up the bed slowly. When he was close enough, Nick grabbed him and pulled him down. Rion assumed he was going to continue to be aggressive, but instead, Nick gave him sensual kisses, his tongue gently caressing Rion's lips and the inside of his mouth. Rion straddled Nick and kissed him back with the same sweet intensity, moving his body slightly up and down against him, Nick's cock sliding in between the crack of Rion's bottom. Nick sat all the way up, rubbed his back, and held him tight, savoring the feel of his full lips, drinking his saliva that slid off Rion's tongue into his mouth. Heat and electricity flowed through their bodies from their mouths, and they couldn't stop kissing each other. Not until both their torsos were wet with pre-cum and Nick's cock head was purple and aching.

"Please," Nick whispered in between kisses. "Let me be inside of you. Please, Ree."

Instead of responding, Rion kissed his face, reached over, and grabbed the lube and the condoms. He placed the lube in Nick's hand but held onto the condoms. He looked at them between his fingers, then looked down at Nick and cocked his head to the side questioningly. It took Nick less than a moment to figure out what he was offering.

"Oh God, yes," Nicholas said, nodding his head profusely, his eyes wide, his heart pounding.

Rion snorted in laughter and tossed them over the bed. He laid down on his side and turned his back to him. Nick had to take a moment to compose himself. The anticipation was greater than ever before. He pushed Rion over slightly and pumped gel onto his fingers, then gently put two inside of his lover. Rion groaned. Nick did it again and again, opening him up, and getting him as lubricated as possible before he added lube to himself. He took a deep breath to calm himself down again, then held onto the base of his cock, closed his eyes, and guided it inside of Rion. Then he laid down beside him.

Rion moaned loudly and arched his back. He was very tight, so Nick moved incredibly slowly, never wanting the feel of the first time unsheathed to end. All too soon, he felt his hair on Rion's bottom, and there was nowhere left to go. Nick reached down and pulled the comforter up and around them. Rion took Nick's hand off his waist and pulled it to his chest, lacing his fingers and squeezing tightly. Nick knew Rion needed a moment, and he did, too. Together they laid connected as one and breathed in sync.

Nick kissed the back of Rion's curly hair, pulled back halfway, then sank himself back inside. Rion moaned loudly again. Nick let a breath pass, then did it again. "God, Nicky!" Rion called out.

Nick dug his nose into Rion's hair and began to move slightly faster, pacing himself like the waves across the sand. He focused on the sound of Rion's moaning, the beat of his own heart against Rion's back, and the feel of Rion's tight, wet anus squeezing the flesh of his cock. Nick didn't know how he had been able to keep his orgasm at bay for so long, but eventually, he found himself moving faster, pushing harder, until he began to see colors behind his closed eyes and released. Nothing had ever felt more perfect.

Nick pulled out steadily and fell onto his back. As he was still coming down from his climax, he felt Rion get on top of him. He opened his eyes slightly to see Rion's smirk. Nick was still hard, and Rion took full advantage, sitting on his chest and sliding his cock back inside.

"Holy shit, Rion," Nick breathed out.

"Shhh..." he said softly. "Enjoy the ride." And with that, Rion began to move.

Nick was incredibly sensitive and found himself moaning loudly, holding onto Rion's thighs. Rion rocked back and forth and fucked himself on Nick's cock, his hands on Nick's shoulders, moaning liberally.

Nick relinquished all control as his orgasm built up in his body again, quicker than last time.

"Rion... Rion... Rion... Rion..." he called his name repeatedly as his eyes crossed, his body seized, and more cum spurted out of his cock into Rion's body.

Rion kept riding until his own orgasm hit him hard. "Mmmmm, Nicky," Rion moaned out, and white strings of cum began to pump out of his untouched cock right onto Nick's chest. He continued to bounce. Nicky grabbed Rion's cock and began to tug, squeezing cum out. Rion cried out; Nick's touch was painful and pleasurable at the same time.

"I'm sensitive; stop," Rion moaned again.

"You stop moving first," Nick groaned.

Rion stopped moving and slid off Nick's body to lay next to him. Neither of them could move. They laid there, staring at the ceiling, breathing hard through their mouths, smiles plastered across their faces. Rion reached over first, running his hands through Nick's hairy chest, mixing in his cum and Nick's sweat, making Nick laugh. Nick turned to his side and took Rion's hand. Looking him in the eyes, he put each finger in his mouth and sucked them one by one. When he had finished with all five, Rion leaned in, mouth opened. Nick responded by meeting their tongues, and they kissed intensely again, running their fingers through each other's hair, pressing their bodies together.

"I think you tried to break my dick," Nick said in between kisses.

"You squeezed the life out of mine," Rion said back.

Nick murmured against his cheek, "Is it crazy that I want to be inside of you again, but I don't think my dick will cooperate?"

Rion laughed. "Sorry for just... taking it. I just... had to."

"Don't ever be sorry with me," Nicholas told him. "Everything about tonight was perfect."

"It was perfect, Nicky," Rion agreed.

They laid together, staring at each other, but he could tell Rion was trying to keep his eyes open. "Sleep, Ree. I'll be here in the morning."

Rion smiled. "I'll be here the day after that, too."

Nick smiled back. "So you've decided already? Maybe wait until the morning. See how you feel about us being together. You may get the urge to get on a plane and go back home."

Rion shook his head. "I didn't buy a return ticket."

Nick let a few moments go by. "Why not?"

"I'm staying at an Airbnb in Chelsea until I find an apartment or a roommate. I already sublet my apartment in San Francisco to a friend of Ava's, and Muriel has my Jeep. I had decided the moment I booked my ticket, Nicky. I'm staying in New York. So you'll always have access to me."

Nick looked up at the ceiling, then back down at him. "You didn't think to tell me that hours ago at dinner? When I kept asking you, 'Why are you here?'"

"I didn't know if you wanted me to stay," Rion replied honestly. "I just needed to know that you wanted to be with me, too, as much as I wanted to be with you."

Nick moved his hand from around Rion's back and began to trace letters on Rion's chest. "N. W. A. W. R."

Rion smiled and kissed his lips. Then he moved farther down and put his face in Nick's chest hair. Nick kissed the top of his head and breathed in deeply. The feel of Rion's slow breath against him, his hands around his body, and the smell of their lovemaking in the air put Nick in a deep sleep.

Nick's alarm went off at 6 a.m. He was on his back, and Rion stirred on his chest. He reached out his hand to turn it off. Rion moved up to kiss his neck but fell back to sleep just as quickly. It made Nick smile. He rubbed Rion's back rhythmically and held onto him for another thirty minutes, thinking about nothing, happiness flooding through him. Eventually, he moved Rion's hand from around him and adjusted his body to gently put his boyfriend onto the silk sheets and mattress. Rion sighed a bit, but continued to sleep.

Nick kissed his face before getting off the bed and going into his shower. He took his time while washing, thinking about New Year's Eve's plans, only four days away. Originally, he had planned to sit at home alone, but now that Rion was there, he would take him to the New Year's Eve party that Zoey had set up for him to attend, where other famous people would be there, all for publicity purposes. Or maybe if Rion wanted to spend it at home, he would do that, too. Whatever he wanted.

Nick came out of the shower to his closet to pull out his clothes for the day. Once dressed, he came into the bedroom, and Rion was still asleep. *He sleeps like the dead*, Nick thought with a smile.

Nick walked over to him and ran his fingers through his hair. "Ree."

"Hmmm," Rion responded without moving or opening up his eyes.

"I have to go to work."

"Um-hmm," he replied.

"I should be back around 4 p.m."

"Mm'kay," he mumbled.

Nick was thoughtful. He left the room and went into the kitchen, taking his ring of extra keys out of the junk drawer, and walked back to the room.

"Rion." He said his name a little more loudly.

"Hmmm?"

"Wake up." Rion sighed and opened his eyes slightly but didn't move his body. "Where did you say you were staying again?"

"Hmmm... Airbnb in Chelsea."

"Hm," Nick responded.

He took the gold key off his ring and tossed it onto the bed. It landed right next to Rion's face. That woke him up completely. Rion leaned onto his elbows and touched the key.

"Nick—" Rion started to say.

Nick cut him off. "So you're not beholden to me. So you can go and come as you please. So you know that you always have a home and a place to lay your head." Rion didn't respond. He continued to rub the key with his finger. "If you still want your own space later, that's fine. But for now, go get your stuff, Rion."

"Okay," he said softly. Nick came to the bed and kissed his head. As he turned back, he heard Rion say in a clear voice, "I love you, Nicholas."

Nick turned around, and Rion was staring at him with the most adoring brown eyes. He bent back down as Rion raised his head, and they kissed softly. "I love you, too, Rion." He kissed his lips again and then headed out of the bedroom.

Nick put on his heavy winter jacket, winter boots, wool hat, and leather gloves. He went down to the lobby, and the attendant held the door open for him. It had just started to snow, but it wasn't sticking yet, just making the gray sidewalk wet. He stood there and looked over the Hudson River, icy but still flowing, wondering if Rion had ever seen snow before today. Probably not, having lived in Fresno and San Francisco his whole life.

*He's gonna love the view of the snow falling when he wakes up*, Nick thought happily. *Rion is going to love it here with me*. It was cold, the wind biting as flurries floated around. But Nick had a warmth in his chest that spread throughout his body.

The doorman came over to him. "Mr. Highton? Did you need something? Need me to have the valet bring your car around?"

Nick took a moment to answer. "It's such a beautiful day, Adam. I'm going to walk. Thank you."

Nicholas turned to smile at the old man and headed southbound to his office, approximately twenty city blocks away.

# BOOK CLUB QUESTIONS

1. Nick and Rion instantly felt comfortable enough with each other to talk about their personal thoughts and feelings about their families and their lives. Have you ever met someone and instantly felt connected to them?

2. How are Nicholas and Rion different? How are they similar?

3. In what ways has Nick's fame and fortune been positive? How has it negatively affected his life?

4. Rion has a family history of addiction. How has this shaped his life and view of the world?

5. Many minor characters were introduced: Parker, Kaleb, Sonny, Lennox, Rilianne, Laurence, and Penelope. Which character would you like to see more of?

6. When Nick returned to London, Rion listed all the reasons they should not be together. Did he have a point? Why or why not?

7. Do any of the characters remind you of real-life people or celebrities?

8. What chapter would you point out as the pivotal moment for Rion? For Nick?

9. What do you think will happen next to the main characters?

10. Have you read any other books by this author? How would you compare them to this selection?

# AUTHOR BIO

*W*ife, mother, partner, daughter, sister, friend, social worker, life skills coach, and part-time erotic romance novelist, Eskay Kabba finds the complexity of human nature and creates romantic and erotic love stories. The characters reflect the notion that no one is all good or all bad, but we are all just trying to find love in hard places. Eskay pens erotic romance novels that celebrates the LGBTQ community, people of color, and interracial relationships. When not writing about the throes of passion, Eskay finds joy in spending time with her family and loved ones, reading dystopia and fantasy series, and bingeing popular shows from a streaming app. Eskay. Kabba@gmail.com

# More books from
## 4 Horsemen Publications

## LGBT Romance

### AJ Buchannan
Orchestrated Love

Mikaél's Moment: Type 6
Stephan's Resurgence: Type 5
Anastasia's Arrival: Type 6

### Eskay Kabba
Hidden Love
Not So Hidden
Signs of Affection
Deeply Devoted to Him
Honest Love
A Plane and Simple Connection

### Stormie Skyes
Check Yes, No, or Maybe

### V.C. Willis
The Prince's Priest
The Priest's Assassin
The Assassin's Saint
The Champion's Lord

### Lucas LaMont
Roman's Reckoning: Type 6

## LGBT Erotica

### Dominic N. Ashen
Steel & Thunder
Storms & Sacrifice
Secrets & Spires
Arenas & Monsters
My Three Orc Dads: a Novella
Before the Storm: a Novella

### Grayson Ace
How I Got Here
First Year Out of the Closet
You're Only a Top?
You're Only a Bottom?
I Think I'm a Serial Swiper
Lookin in All the Wrong Places
What Makes Me a Whore?
A Breach in Confidentiality
Back Door Pass
My European Adventure
An Unexpected Affair
Finding True Love
The Dr. Cage Chronicles

### Eskay Kabba
Hidden Love
Not So Hidden
Signs of Affection
Deeply Devoted to Him
Honest Love
A Plane and Simple Connection

www.ingramcontent.com/pod-product-compliance
Lightning Source LLC
Chambersburg PA
CBHW020131120726
47903CB00007B/2212